# PRAISE FOR THE

Here are some of the over 10(
Dead Cold Mystery series.

"Rex Stout and Michael Connelly have spawned a protege."

"So begins one damned fine read."

"Mystery that's more brain than brawn."

"I read so many of this genre...and ever so often I strike gold!"

"This book is filled with action, intrigue, espionage, and everything else lovers of a good thriller want."

# UNNATURAL MURDER

A DEAD COLD MYSTERY

**BLAKE BANNER**

R

RIGHTHOUSE

ISBN-13: 978-1-63696-008-1

ISBN-10: 1-63696-008-1

Cover design by: Damonza

Printed in the United States of America

www.righthouse.com

www.instagram.com/righthousebooks

www.facebook.com/righthousebooks

twitter.com/righthousebooks

# ONE

WHEN YOU SEE IT ON TV, IT HAS DRAMA. BUT IN THE real, three-dimensional world, the steady throb of the red-and-blue lights in the darkness, the way they wash the walls of the house with their dull colors, the way they make the black windows look hollow and empty, like dead eyes—that has no drama. And the pain and the convulsive weeping of the girl who loved the victim and now sees him lifeless and gaping behind the wheel of his cheap Toyota, the numb, expressionless faces of the uniforms who have seen it all before, the ME and the CSI team, who just want to go home to bed—all of that, all of it, it has no drama. The true horror of that scene, of all the scenes like it, lies in the fact that it is banal, it is horrifically ordinary.

We climbed out of Dehan's Focus and ducked under the yellow tape that hung across Bryant Avenue, segregating two houses from the rest of the world, because here somebody had been killed, murdered. Sergeant Solano met us as we crossed the line. Dehan was frowning at him; at three a.m., she'd brought her attitude with her.

"You want to explain to me why I'm here, Sergeant?"

Solano made a face like sheepish turning to worried and said, "I wasn't sure what to do, Detective. It's three a.m. and the inspector's not at the station. It ain't a cold case exactly, but it might be connected. And I knew you . . . your mom . . . So I told Dispatch . . ."

He trailed off. The expression on Dehan's face might have made Godzilla trail off. It made intimidating look like a welcome respite. So I said, "You did the right thing, Sergeant. Walk us through it."

He gave me a grateful smile and pointed at the Toyota. It was parked under a streetlamp. I glanced at what lay beyond it: a run-down, terraced house with steps rising to a large veranda behind wrought iron railings, a redbrick wall and peeling green paint on a cheap door and a window frame; a girl, Latina, sitting on a wooden chair, in her twenties, barefoot, wearing shorts and a T-shirt, crying; a female cop hunkered down by her side, trying to comfort somebody who can never be comforted.

Dehan had moved to the window of the car and was peering in. I said to Solano, "Okay, what's the story?"

"Two victims, Detective." He moved toward the vehicle and I went and stood beside Dehan, looking through the shattered window. There was a young man, maybe midtwenties. He was slumped over on his right side. He looked uncomfortable. There was a lot of blood from two bullet wounds in his head, and at least three more in his arm and chest.

Solano was saying, "This is Sebastian Acosta, resident at the Jacobi . . ."

On the other side of the car, crouching by the passenger seat in the open doorway, I could see Frank, the ME, looking back at me. "Good morning, Frank."

"I knew them." He said it in a dead voice that masked his anger.

I turned back to Solano. "Thanks, Sergeant. I'll give you a shout if I need you. You canvassing the neighbors?"

"Yeah, we're on it."

"Okay, I'll talk to you in a minute."

Dehan had moved around the car. Frank stood, and I joined

them. There was blood on the sidewalk and on the stairs leading up to the veranda. Frank looked unhappy.

"Sebastian Acosta, twenty-six, wanted to be an ME." He pointed at the blood on the stairs. "His friend, Luis Irizarry, twenty-five, was going to be a plastic surgeon. He said there was more money in it and you didn't have to watch your patients die."

Dehan voiced the question I was wondering. "Where is he?"

"In a coma, in an ambulance on his way to the Jacobi."

She screwed up her face. "They were both residents?"

He nodded. "They'd been through med school together and they were doing their residency together."

I asked, "How bad is Luis?"

"Pretty bad. We won't know till he gets there. He took two rounds to the chest. Sebastian took the brunt of the attack. He has two shots to the head and three to the body, point blank. There are powder burns on his face." He pulled out his cell. "I'll get Personnel to email you their addresses."

I walked back around to the driver's side and stood where the shooter must have stood, with my arms outstretched as though I was holding a gun. Dehan came and stood beside me.

"I think I remember them."

I glanced at her. "Yeah?"

She nodded. "And that girl." She jerked her head at the veranda. "I think she's Rosario's daughter, Angela."

"Rosario?"

"My mom's friend. Rosario Rojas. That's what Solano was talking about. Rosario was raped and murdered in this house. That's her daughter. When they were kids, she used to hang out with these two."

"How'd Solano know?"

She raised an eyebrow at me. "Station-house gossip. We are paid to snoop, Stone."

I made a face. "I guess you're right. You okay with this?"

"Sure. I'm going to talk to Angela."

The female police officer had given up on her attempts to

console her and now just stood by her side. As we approached, Dehan asked the cop, "Has she made a statement?"

The officer shook her head. "I'm afraid not, Detective."

Dehan nodded. "Okay, we've got this."

She hunkered down in front of Angela and I rested my ass on the wrought iron railing. Angela looked away. Her face was wet with tears and her bottom lip was trembling. Dehan said, "Hey, Angela, you remember me?"

She looked at her sidelong for a moment, then shook her head.

Dehan smiled. "My mom was Marta. She was a real close friend of your mom's."

"Marta . . . ?"

"Yeah." She pointed up toward Garrison Avenue. "We lived up on the corner of Garrison and Faile. We had the café. You remember? My mom was always over here, having coffee with Rosario."

She nodded. "Yeah, I remember."

"Did you make the call?"

Angela nodded.

"Okay, let's get you dressed and take you down to the station. C'mon, I'll give you a hand."

She led her inside and a light came on in the window. I sat a moment, looking at the door. About two feet from the bottom there were what looked like two bullet holes. I logged the fact for later consideration, stood, and looked down at the scene in the street. I wondered where the gunman had come from. I caught Solano's eye and called him up.

He was talking as he climbed the steps. "We got two 911 calls within less than a minute of each other. We were already on the way when the second call came through, reporting shots fired. From what we can make out, the victims arrived, the shooter must have been waiting, approached the car, and fired through the window. Five of the seven shots hit the driver, two hit the passenger. He got out and tried to make it to the house but collapsed on the stairs. Then the shooter must have taken off, because we got here very shortly afterwards."

"What do the neighbors say?"

He sighed and looked apologetic. "So far a few people heard shots—between five and seven—but nobody saw nothing." He shrugged. "This kind of neighborhood . . ."

"I know, Sergeant, there is not a lot of trust. Between five and seven, huh? Okay, you called Crime Scene?"

"They're on their way."

He left, and I went and pushed open the door. It gave onto a hallway with a broad, wooden staircase rising along the right wall and a passage on the left that gave onto a front room, a back room, and a kitchen. I walked back down the steps to the sidewalk. I counted nine of them. Then I turned and faced the door, holding out my arm like I was shooting. The angle was wrong, so I lay down on the road. A couple of the uniforms looked at me and smiled. I ignored them and held out my arm again, like I was shooting from a prone position. After that, I got to my feet again and climbed back to the hall. There I got on my knees and inspected the wall. After a moment I found what I was looking for, a bullet hole. But I only found one.

Outside, the crime scene team had arrived, and I walked down to meet them. Joe, the team leader, was suiting up at the back of their van.

"Stone. I thought you only did cold cases these days."

"Yeah, so did I. Listen, looks like the crime scene is out here, but do me a favor, will you? Have a look at the door. There are two bullet holes at about two feet. Inside, slightly to the left, there is one bullet hole in the wall. To me, none of it looks fresh. I'd like to know how old they are and what caliber we're looking at."

He nodded. "Sure, no problem. Say . . ." He smiled. "How's things with your partner? Still teamed up with Detective Dehan?"

I raised an eyebrow. "Yeah, why?"

He grinned. "Just making polite conversation, John. I'll catch you later."

I watched him walk away toward the car, followed by the three members of his team, all in white plastic suits, like B-movie aliens. He gestured with his hand and said something, and one of them climbed the stairs as Dehan and Angela came out the old, peeling green door.

They joined me and Dehan asked, "We done here?"

I looked up and down the road, still trying to work out where the shooter came from. There were plenty of spaces where a car could have parked. I walked away so I was standing in front of the Toyota, about five yards distant. The streetlamps made an amber glow on the windshield. There was a look of desolation about it.

"Solano!"

He turned to look at me.

I pointed at the car. "Was the engine running?"

"No, Detective. It was just like that when we arrived."

I walked to the nearest space behind the car. Then I looked across at the other side of the road, where a steel fence blocked off a stretch of overgrown garden. Every parking space on that side was occupied. I stared at Dehan. She was watching me, with her right hand on Angela's arm. I said, "Okay, let's go."

Back at the station, we put Angela in interview room three and went to get some coffee. At the machine, I leaned against the wall while Dehan filled the polystyrene cups.

"Did you notice the holes in the door?"

She glanced at me. "No."

"Joe's having a look at them for me. They're low down, about mid-shin. Two of them. Aside from that, any initial thoughts?"

She frowned and leaned against the wall opposite me. "Yeah. The shooter knew his victims, knew their car, it was kind of an execution, but he was real mad too."

I nodded. "Knew them why?"

"Because I watched you. You were checking if you could see in through the windshield, or the side window. He would not have been able to see their faces from the front because of the glare from the streetlamps, or the back simply because it's impossible.

And from where he stood to shoot, unless he was a dwarf, their faces were hidden by the roof of the car. Plus, he shot through a closed window, which, under the lamp, would have made it doubly hard to see them. Ergo, he knew who they were, and he knew their car. Obviously he was waiting for them, popped them when they arrived, and then made off."

I nodded. "What about Angela?"

She shrugged. "I was thinking maybe she's just a random witness. You know . . ." She spread her hands. "Med students, access to chemical substances, tempted to help pay their fees with a little private enterprise. Maybe they thought they were meeting a buyer and instead they met with somebody whose toes they were treading on."

I sucked my teeth. "Mm-hm, that crossed my mind too. And they just happened to meet outside her house."

"But your bullet holes in the door suggest the connection might be more than that." She hesitated a moment. "Especially as they knew each other."

"I agree. Witnesses in the street say they heard between five and seven shots. There were seven shots in the victims. The two in the door would have made it nine. I found a bullet hole in the wall, but no slugs."

"Just one?"

I nodded, then shrugged. "Suggests somebody got injured, but there was no blood. I'm pretty sure those two shots were not fired tonight. If I'm right, there ought to be a police report. I'm interested to hear what Angela has to say about it."

We stared at each other for a long moment. Then she gave a small smile and said, "Let's find out."

# TWO

She didn't look at us as we sat down. Dehan placed the cup of coffee in front of her and smiled.

"It's not exactly coffee, but it's hot and sweet and it will help with the shock."

Angela nodded but still didn't make eye contact. After a moment, she said, "Will I be able to go home soon?"

Dehan didn't answer for a moment, then she said, "Of course, whenever you like, but we need to get a statement from you. It shouldn't take long."

Angela went to speak, stopped, then said, "I didn't really see anything."

I scratched my head. "Did you make the 911 call?"

She nodded.

I went on, "What made you call?"

"I heard shooting."

"How many shots did you hear?"

She fiddled with her fingertips, looking at her coffee, like she hoped it would tell her how many shots she'd heard. After a bit, she shrugged. "I don't know."

I bobbed my head slowly a few times, like I was thinking. "More than one?"

"Yeah. More than one."

"Less than twelve?" She nodded again. I went on. "More than three?"

"Yes."

"Less than, say, ten?"

She gave a small sigh and reached for the coffee. "Probably five or six."

"Good, that's very helpful, Angela. Now I'd like to ask you something else. Did the shots come all together, kind of *bang, bang, bang*! Or were they spaced out?"

"All together, like, one after another, real quick. Like, one two three, one two three, and then one. So I guess it was seven."

I smiled at her. "That's very good. That's excellent. Were you in bed?"

"Yes."

"What made you realize that they were shots?"

Now she stared at me, real hard, and swallowed a couple of times. "I don't know what you mean."

I spread my hands. "I'm just trying to get a picture of what happened. You're in bed and you hear what sounds like seven firecrackers going off in rapid succession, right . . . ?"

She gave a very small nod and half-whispered, "Yes . . ."

"And you didn't go and look to see what it was, you immediately went to the phone . . ."

Dehan added, "Downstairs."

"So you must have known they were gunshots. I was just wondering how you knew they were gunshots."

She looked like she was about to start crying again. She started to speak two or three times but stopped herself, and finally said, "Well, I looked *quickly* out of the window."

I smiled kindly. "Oh, that's great. So you did see *something*, just—not very much."

"Yes."

"So you heard the shots, you got out of bed, and peered

quickly out of the window. What did you see that made you call 911?"

Her bottom lip was trembling and tears spilled from her eyes. She covered her mouth with her hands. I reached into my pocket for a handkerchief and handed it to her.

"There is no hurry, Angela. I know this has been very traumatic. We would just really like to get whoever did this to . . ." I frowned at Dehan, like I couldn't remember their names.

Dehan reached across the table and took Angela's hand. "Hey, listen, take it easy. In your own time." She smiled. "What were their names? I remember you guys used to play together, right?"

It was like a trigger. She went to pieces, sobbing violently into my handkerchief, making the ugly, convulsive noises of deep grief. Dehan stood and pulled her chair around so she was sitting next to her, and put her arm around her shoulder. The sobbing lasted a good four or five minutes. Eventually, Dehan persuaded her to have some of the coffee, and that seemed to settle her a bit. Then Dehan said, "Hey, we can do this a little later. Maybe we can come 'round in the afternoon and take a statement from you." She looked at me and I nodded. "But, before we take you back, can you just give me a *rough* idea of what you saw when you looked out of the window?"

Angela stared at the tabletop, but like she wasn't seeing it, like she was seeing something else instead, something that made her scared. Her breathing was ragged. Finally, she said, "There was just a man running to his car. Seb was lying on the seat and Luis was on the steps. The man got in his car and drove away."

I said, "Was his car on your right or on your left?"

"On the right."

"And once you saw that, you ran downstairs and dialed 911?"

She nodded.

I looked at Dehan. "I don't know if you have any more questions, Detective Dehan. I have all I need for now."

Dehan gave Angela a squeeze and said, "We will need a full

statement later on, but right now I'll get somebody to drive you home. You need me to call anyone? A doctor, a friend?"

"No. I'm fine."

They got up and moved to the door. As she was about to leave the room, I had a thought. "Angela?" She stopped and looked at me like she was afraid I was going to make her stand in the naughty corner. "Do you think whoever did this saw you at the window?"

She stared at me for a long while before she shook her head. After that, Dehan walked her downstairs and I made my way to our desks. There I dropped into my chair and sat gazing at the black window that showed nothing of the creeping dawn, but just the orange wash of the streetlamp on the corner of Story Avenue. Dehan came in on her long legs, yawning, and fell into the chair opposite me, leaning her elbows on the desk. We stared at each other for a while and eventually, I said, "From her bedroom window, she could not have seen Sebastian lying across the seat. Neither could she have seen Luis on the stairs."

She chewed her lip and gave three ponderous nods. "She was downstairs."

"I think you are right. First order of priority, Carmen, we need to find out what those boys were doing there at three in the morning. I don't believe it is a coincidence that they were outside her house. They were close friends, you could see that by the way she went to pieces when you mentioned they used to play together."

"I noticed that."

"They were there . . ." I shrugged. "They were there for *her*, for some reason. Which begs the question, how did the shooter know they were going to be there?"

"I told Angela we'd see her again after she'd had time to sleep and get over the shock. She said she'd take a pill." She looked at her watch. "It's just after four. We should go and call on the parents."

I sighed and rubbed my face. "Yes . . ."

"You want me to take Acosta and you . . ."

I interrupted her. "No. I'd like us both to do both. This is going to be a complicated case. My gut tells me there will be subtle emotional nuances all over the damned place. I want you there so we can discuss it. We'll see Luis' family first, then Sebastian's."

"You got it, Sensei."

We took her car because my Jaguar was still at my house. She had picked me up after Dispatch called her. I climbed in the passenger seat and slammed the door. She fired up the engine, and I looked at her profile against the creeping light of early dawn. She was exquisite, and totally unaware of it.

She backed out onto Fteley Avenue and headed for Bruckner Boulevard. The Irizarry family lived not far from me, in Morris Park.

"One thing I am still not clear about," I said, as she pulled onto the freeway, "is how this becomes a cold case."

She grimaced. "I've been wondering that myself. I see it and I don't."

"Explain."

She gave a little sigh and thought for a bit. As we turned onto White Plains Road, she started to talk.

"I'm going back a bit. This must be 2004, maybe 2003, so I was thirteen, fourteen. It was about a year before my parents died. My mom had become real close with Rosario, one of the mothers in the barrio."

"Barrio?"

She glanced at me. "Yeah. My mom wasn't an intellectual, but she liked intelligent people. Rosario was smart. She hadn't had much in the way of opportunities or schooling, but she read a lot and she had opinions. She liked my mom because my mom had broken the rules. You know, defied the church, her family, married a Jewish guy. Anyhow, after a while Rosario starts hanging out with a crowd . . ."

She stopped and made a face like she didn't really approve of what she was going to say. I prompted her, "A crowd? What kind of crowd?"

"My dad described them as 'fast.' My mom wasn't crazy about them either. From what I remember"—she glanced at me again—"and I was only about fourteen years old! From what I remember, there were two couples. One of them was mixed race, which attracted a lot of attention. She was a white academic." She laughed. "She might have been a schoolteacher for all I know! But that was the impression. Radical left wing, making a statement, you know the kind of thing."

I managed to frown and raise an eyebrow at the same time. "Kind of woman who made it possible for you to have your job."

"Absolutely. I'm not criticizing. Shut up and listen. Anyhow, she was married to a black guy, black Puerto Rican, I think. He was also some kind of academic. I remember there was some talk about him being ill, and he may have died. These two were close friends with another couple . . ." She thought for a moment. "Eddie and Maria. This couple were also Puerto Rican. He was a defense attorney. He was just starting out, but he was doing okay. He was becoming successful. I don't remember anything about his wife, except that Mom used to say it was a shame he didn't look out for her rights as much as he did for the crooks he helped set free. That was my mom all over. So those four used to hang out, have barbeques and talk the good talk."

"And these are . . . ?"

She seemed to nod with her whole body while she spoke. "These are the parents of our vics. Now, shut up while I tell you. Mom never hung out with them. They invited her to a couple of barbeques but she never went. And after a while, she stopped hanging out so much with Rosario, because, she said, there was too much *cuchi cuchi*."

"*Cuchi cuchi* . . . ?"

"Hanky-panky."

"So what, there was wife-swapping going on . . . ?"

She raised an eyebrow at me. "Or husband-swapping. I don't

know, Mom was never more specific. She was pretty straitlaced, and it may have been no more than flirting while drunk. Point is, it only took Rosario telling her about a couple of these get-togethers, and Mom stopped seeing her so much."

"So what happened?"

"Give me a chance and I'll tell you. Next thing, Mom doesn't hear from Rosario for a while, it might have been a couple of weeks, I'm not sure, and suddenly she turns up dead. Turns out, according to the cops, she's been raped and murdered."

"And they never caught who did it."

"Not even a suspect."

"And Angela is Rosario's daughter. Where's the dad?"

"She was a widow. I don't remember her husband. He left her a pension or something."

"And she was killed in that house?"

She looked at me and nodded. "In that same house."

I looked out at the limpid light and the sleepy storefronts of Morris Avenue. Sunrise was still an hour away and the cars and the streetlamps seemed to be hung with amber dreams, still warm from the beds where people slept behind dark windows. For a moment, I envied those sleeping bodies. And then I pitied the two we were going to wake, to tell them their son was in the hospital, shot in the chest.

Outside Rosario's house.

"They're connected. That is a simple fact." I turned toward Dehan. Her face was momentarily washed with orange light, then went into shadow again. "But the connection doesn't seem to mean anything. It may well be that the people are connected, but the crimes are not. If they are not, this is not a cold case."

She sighed, then shrugged. "So we inform the families, make some initial inquiries, report to the inspector later this morning, and see what he says."

I nodded absently. My brain said that made sense. My gut said my brain didn't know what it was talking about.

# THREE

WE PULLED INTO HERING AVENUE. I SAID SOMETHING about it being a fishy address, but Dehan didn't laugh. It was a broad, attractive street with large, detached houses and well-tended front lawns. She pulled up outside a double-fronted redbrick with two horse chestnuts standing guard by some stone steps that made a path through a slightly over-ornate garden. We looked at each other. Dehan heaved a big sigh and we got out. The doors slammed and echoed in the stillness. We climbed the steps to a white door and I leaned on the bell several times. After a minute, a sash window opened above, and an angry voice shouted down.

"Who the hell is it? Get the hell out of here or I'll call the cops!"

I stepped back out into view and looked up at him. I held my badge so he could see it.

"Detectives Stone and Dehan, sir. Are you Eduardo Irizarry?"

He scowled. He was a thickset man of about forty, with a balding head, hairy shoulders, and dark, Hispanic features.

"I am he," he said, rather pompously. "What the hell is this about? Can't it wait to a more civilized hour?"

Hell was a word he seemed to like. I thought sourly that it was a place he was soon going to become familiar with.

"Mr. Irizarry, we need to talk to you, in private . . ." I looked with meaning up and down the street.

He hesitated.

I said, "It's about your son . . ."

He closed the window, and after a moment, a light showed through the glass panels in the front door. Next thing, the door opened to reveal Ed Irizarry wearing a silk dressing gown and a foul expression.

"What the hell is this about?"

I tried to suppress the anger that was beginning to warm my belly but failed. I said, brutally, "Your son has been shot. He is in the hospital in a critical state, but we can come back at a more civilized hour if it's inconvenient now."

Dehan's eyebrows rose high on her forehead and she turned to stare at me. Irizarry went a pasty gray color. "Good God . . . shot? By whom . . . ?"

"Do you think we can come in, sir? This is probably not something you want to discuss in front of all your neighbors."

He nodded once, then again several times and stepped back. "Yes, yes, of course . . . Come in."

He led us through a large, middle-class house that was in fancy dress, pretending to be a rococo palace. Evidently we weren't the kind of people he would have in any of his drawing rooms, so he led us to the kitchen, which was not so much rococo as *Fresh Prince of Bel-Air*. He switched on the lights and stood staring at us with his mouth slightly open, like he'd expected us to be somebody else when the lights came on.

After a moment, I said, "Mr. Irizarry, perhaps you should get your wife."

He frowned. "Mary?"

"Is that your wife's name?"

"Yes, of course it is!"

I nodded. "Then that is who you should get. She needs to hear this. Do you mind if we sit down?"

"Of course . . ."

He turned and walked away, back into the sleeping shadows of his house. The kitchen was brightly lit. The walls were lemon yellow, a vast refrigerator gleamed silver, and there was a large, round pine table with four pine chairs in the middle of a floor laid with big terra-cotta tiles. In the center of the table, there was a bowl brimming with tropical fruit. We sat and waited. I wondered, bizarrely, if he'd notice if I had a banana.

The sound of rushing, unsteady feet on the stairs drove the thought from my mind. We stood as they came back in. Mary was small and dark, perhaps a couple of years younger than her husband. Her hair was in curlers, and she had a dressing gown drawn tight around her, as though she hoped it might protect her somehow. She ran across the kitchen, clutching her gown with her left hand, reaching out to me with her right.

"What's happened? Is he all right? Where is he?"

Eduardo announced in a voice that was too loud, "I'll make coffee!" and stared at us each in turn. I ignored him and guided Mary to a chair. We sat, and Eduardo left the coffeepot by the sink and came to sit with us. He looked for a moment as though he might start weeping.

I put my fists on the table and spoke. "Mrs. Irizarry, Mr. Irizarry, we do not know all the details yet, but in the early hours of this morning, at about three o'clock, Luis and his friend Sebastian were parked in a car in Hunts Point . . ."

Eduardo's eyes went wide. "*Hunts Point? What the hell . . . ?*"

Mary covered her ears and screwed up her face. "Ed, *please*!" It was an eloquent gesture that spoke of a hypersensitivity developed over years of enduring his unquenchable outrage at everything he encountered.

I ignored them both and went on. "It seems they were approached by an unidentified person and shot point-blank. Luis was in the passenger seat and managed to exit the car. He received two bullet wounds to the chest. He is in critical condition at the Jacobi."

Ed's mouth was sagging open. He kept staring around the room, as though he was following a slow-moving fly on its journey around the kitchen. Mary had both hands over her mouth. Her eyes were huge with horror as she stared at my face, struggling to give some meaning to what I had told her.

It was Ed who spoke first. "What was he doing at *Hunts Point*?"

Dehan answered him. "We were hoping you might be able to shed some light on that, Mr. Irizarry."

He glared at her. "*I?* How the hell would I know?"

"Ed, *please*! These people are here to help us . . . !"

"*Cops? Help us?* Just shut up, Mary!" He turned back to Dehan. "I have no idea what he was doing there . . ."

Dehan's eyes were hooded when she cut him short. "There were two of them, Mr. Irizarry. He was with his friend Sebastian. You know Sebastian, don't you?"

Mary said, "They've been friends since they were tiny. Is Sebastian badly hurt?"

"He received five shots. Two to the head and three to his arm and chest. He is dead."

Her face twisted with grief. "Oh no . . ." Her voice was the voice of infinite sadness. She said it again. "Oh, no, no . . . Poor Sue. Poor Sue . . ."

She took a handkerchief from her pocket and began to sob into it. She cried silently, with her shoulders shaking in small spasms. I was struck with the impression that crying silently and unnoticed was something she had learned to do over the years. Dehan turned back to Ed, who was staring at the tabletop.

"The reason we thought you might be able to shed some light on why they were where they were, Mr. Irizarry, is that they were parked outside Rosario's house. You remember Rosario, right?"

He didn't do anything. He didn't react. Only, his eyes stared a little harder, and it was his motionlessness that was so striking.

Mary's sobbing stopped abruptly and she looked up at Dehan. "Rosario . . . ? She's dead . . . !"

"I know, Mrs. Irizarry. That house now belongs to Angela. Have you any idea why Luis and Sebastian would be parked outside Angela's house at three in the morning?"

Ed's eyes narrowed. "What are you implying?"

I put my elbows on the table and leaned forward. "It's a simple question, Mr. Irizarry. We are not implying anything. We know that at one time you were both friends with Rosario, and the boys used to play with Angela. So, have you any idea what they might have been doing there?"

He didn't answer. Mary shook her head. "I thought they had lost touch. When we moved out of the neighborhood, we lost touch with Rosario, Sue, Matt . . ."

I asked, "Sue and Matt were Sebastian's parents?"

She nodded. "Matt was ill. He died. Poor Sue, this is going to hit her so hard."

Dehan sighed. "Please forgive me, we have to ask these questions: Have you any idea, at all, however remote, who might have wanted to hurt Luis and Sebastian?"

Ed snorted. "You can spare us the phony empathy, Detective. The answer is no. And we will not collaborate in your transparent attempts to frame our son as being involved in drugs or prostitution. Whatever that loser Sebastian might have been involved in, I have no idea. But Luis had nothing to do with it!"

"*Ed!*" Mary's face was crimson and her neck taut and corded. She stared at her husband, and before he could answer she half-screamed at him, "*Can you not give it a rest for one single minute? Our son is dying in the hospital and all you can think of is scoring points off poor Sue! Sebastian is dead, for God's sake! Is there no trace of humanity in you?*"

He scowled at the table. The kitchen was strangely still and silent after her outburst. I looked at Dehan. She shook her head.

"Thank you, Mrs. Irizarry, you have been very helpful. We are very sorry to have brought you this news." We stood, and Mary stood with us. Ed continued to stare sullenly at the table, like it was the table's fault he was such an ass.

Dehan went on, "We may need to contact you again, but we'll try to trouble you as little as possible."

Ed snorted, and Mary showed us to the door through the dark house where dark blue light was beginning to tint the glass in the windows. We stepped out into the wild chatter of the dawn chorus. The door closed behind us, and I went and leaned on the car, gazing at the sleeping street under a sky that was turning from midnight blue to gray. The Irizarry house was the only one with lights in the windows. Unlike the squabbling birds, the people of Hering Avenue had not yet started stirring from sleep.

The car bleeped and flashed, and I climbed into the muffled dark. Dehan got in behind the wheel, fired up the engine, and switched on the headlamps. I said, "Evergreen Avenue. It's past the station, on the right, before the river."

"I know where it is." She pulled away. "Doesn't get any easier, huh?"

"Nope."

We drove in silence for a while. Then she asked, "Why do women stay with guys like that?"

"I've often wondered. If you asked her, she'd probably say, when he's nice he's great, and he makes her laugh. Maybe she figures the financial security makes it worthwhile. Or maybe it's some kind of Stockholm syndrome." Then I added with a sour twist, "Or maybe she wouldn't know who to be, if he wasn't there to tell her."

She was quiet for a moment, then said, "Wow."

"Mornings like this, Dehan, I wonder if Captain Jennifer Cuevas wasn't right when she advised me to take early retirement."

She looked at me like I was crazy. "Seriously?"

"If I am married to my job, my job is Ed and I am Mary."

She laughed, and we drove on in silence through the dawn, toward Soundview, toward a woman who was probably still sleeping, unaware that her life had, in the last few hours, disintegrated, unaware that her son was dead, unaware that nothing would ever be the same again.

Dehan's voice broke into my thoughts. "What do you think happened?"

"Hmmm?"

"Their group of *cuchi cuchi* friends. It broke up, they lost touch, stopped having *cuchi cuchi* parties . . ."

We pulled onto the Bruckner Expressway and started accelerating west. A hint of copper touched the sky from the east as the sun crept over the horizon. I spoke almost without thinking, expressing a feeling rather than an idea. I said, "Rosario was killed." I sighed. I felt unaccountably depressed. "That is the starting point. Rosario was killed. That spoiled their swinging scene, the Irizarrys moved, lost touch with their old *cuchi cuchi* friends. But the boys stayed in touch. Maybe they stayed in touch with Angela too. And now, fourteen years later, Sebastian has been killed, maybe twenty feet from where Rosario was." I looked at her face, and she glanced at me. I said, "And Ed and Mary know that's significant for some reason. This is a cold case, Dehan, no doubt about it. A cold case that just started getting hot."

# FOUR

THE INFORMATION I'D RECEIVED FROM THE JACOBI HAD Sebastian Acosta's mother listed as Susanne Mackenzie. We stood outside her house now, on Evergreen Avenue, and stared up at the door. It was a redbrick house on three floors, with a flat roof and a chimney. The bottom floor was a basement and a garage with a ramp leading down to it from the sidewalk. Nine steps led up to a veranda and a front door that had been completely closed in with white wrought iron railings and a white, seven-foot, wrought iron gate. Above that was another floor with three sash windows. The drapes were all closed.

We stood for a good ten minutes on the steps, ringing at the outside bell. Eventually, one of the drapes on an upstairs window opened a few inches, then closed again. I rang some more, and after three or four minutes, the door opened and a tall woman in her forties stepped onto the veranda. She was a redhead. Her skin was very white, with a spray of freckles over her nose and cheeks. Her hair and her green eyes said she had only just woken up. She was wearing jeans and a white T-shirt, and nothing on her feet. She had a good, athletic body and an intelligent face, but somehow she wasn't attractive. You got the feeling she didn't want to be.

She looked at us both through the railings. "Are you cops?"

We showed her our badges. "I'm Detective Stone, Ms. Mackenzie. This is my partner, Detective Dehan. Why do you ask if we're cops? Were you expecting us?"

"No . . ." She sighed. "Maybe. Is it about Sebastian?"

I nodded. "May we come in?"

She opened the gate and stood back. "Is he okay? Has he done something?"

I studied her face a moment. All I saw was anxiety. "We'd better go inside, Ms. Mackenzie."

Her eyes flicked over my face, then looked at Dehan. She led us indoors to an open-plan living room and kitchen. She sat on the sofa. Dehan sat next to her. I glanced around the room. There was one plate in the drying rack by the sink, and one glass. There were three low bookcases with a wide variety of books: fiction and works on psychology and sociology, feminism and civil rights. A bottle of bourbon, a quarter full, stood by a photograph of Sebastian.

I sat in the armchair. She was staring at me. I held her eye and told her, "Ms. Mackenzie, I have some very bad news. I'm afraid your son was shot and killed last night."

For a moment, she went rigid. Her face flushed red, then went dead white. She put her hands to her mouth and screamed. It was loud, shrill, and startling. She stood, and Dehan stood with her. Then she screamed again, three times, covering her face with her hands, trying to articulate the word "no," but making only a horrific, screeching sound of horror and panic.

Dehan tried to take hold of her. Sue turned to face her with huge, staring eyes, pupils reduced to pinpricks. She tottered two steps back, faltered, and collapsed with a horrible, jarring thud on the floor.

I picked her up in my arms with some difficulty. She was heavier than she looked. I laid her out on the sofa, and Dehan went to the kitchen for a glass of water. I heard her rummaging in a couple of cupboards, and she came back with the drink and a spoonful of honey. She touched the honey to her lips, and after a moment Sue opened her eyes. Her pupils were dilated. She stared at me a moment, and as the realization of what had happened dawned on her anew, her face screwed up, and she curled into the fetal position and started to wail, repeating his name over and over.

Eventually, the crying subsided into convulsive sobbing, and after another minute or so, she lay still and quiet. Dehan stayed sitting with her, her hand on her arm, and after a while she asked her, "Do you want us to call your doctor?" Sue shook her head. Dehan went on, "A friend? Somebody who can be with you?"

She looked up at Dehan, seeming to see her for the first time. Then she stared at me and sat up. She said, "Peggy." She pointed at the bookcase, by the photograph and the bourbon. "My phone. Tell her to come please, I need her. She's a homeopath."

Dehan stood, took the phone, and walked into the kitchen, scrolling through the address book. Sue curled herself into the corner of the sofa, staring at an empty space in front of her face for a while. Then she moved her head and stared at a different empty space, like she was seeing something different in each empty space she looked at.

"Ms. Mackenzie." She blinked and looked at me now. "It's important that we get on the trail of whoever did this as quickly as possible. Do you feel up to answering a few questions?"

She stared for a moment. "Like what?"

The question surprised me. I frowned. "When we arrived, you seemed to know that it was about Sebastian . . ."

"He didn't come home last night. I was worried."

"You thought he might have done something."

"Luis. Luis was a bad influence on Sebastian. Sebastian worked so hard, he was doing so well. Luis was always taking him to parties to meet girls. It was probably his fault that this happened . . ."

Her lower lip curled in and she started to cry again. I could hear Dehan talking quietly in the kitchen. I pressed on. "Can you think why Sebastian would have been at Hunts Point last night?"

She didn't answer for a long moment. I was about to repeat the question when she shook her head. "No, of course not."

Dehan returned and sat beside Sue. "Peggy is on her way. She'll be here in about ten minutes."

Sue looked at her but said nothing.

I said, "Ms. Mackenzie, we are almost done, and we really do appreciate your help. Can you think of anyone, however far-fetched, who might have wanted to hurt your son?"

She shook her head. "He was the nicest, sweetest, kindest . . ." Again she covered her face with her hands and started to cry. I glanced at Dehan. She put her arm around her and stroked her back and shoulders.

"What about friends, colleagues at the hospital, is there anyone we can talk to?"

Mary had my handkerchief. I stood and went to the kitchen, found a roll of paper, and brought it back. I handed it to Sue. She took it and blew her nose, then wiped her eyes. "Elizabeth," she said. "Elizabeth Kelly. An intern he was seeing at the hospital. They weren't that serious. I haven't got a number. What happened? How did it happen? What was he doing in Hunts Point?"

"That is something we are trying to find out. They had parked on Bryant Avenue . . ." I paused to see if she would react. She just stared at me, so I went on. "An unknown person approached the car and shot them."

Her face clenched in on itself. Her lip curled in. She curled in, tucking her elbows into her belly, silently swaying from side to side. The howl of pain didn't come for maybe fifteen or twenty seconds. And then it was an awful sound. The doorbell rang, and I rose gratefully to open it.

There was a middle-aged woman in sensible clothes, holding a bag and looking at me as though she was ready to blame me for something, anything, most things. I said, "Are you Peggy?"

"Yes, I am. Where is she?"

I stood back. "On the sofa."

She bustled through, opening her bag as she went.

"All right, you can leave now. There will be no questions and no answers today! You have caused quite enough upset as it is, *thank* you!"

I looked at Dehan and sighed. "Peggy, this is a murder inquiry. We will have to come back and ask Ms. Mackenzie some questions. Will you please let us know when she is able to see us?"

She looked at me, pointed at the door, and said, "Please close it on your way out, Detective."

I took a card out of my wallet and put it on the coffee table, and we left.

Outside, it was a bright morning. I looked at my watch. It was thirty minutes after six.

"I need a gallon of coffee and some breakfast. What do you say we head over to the hospital, see if Elizabeth Kelly is around, and grab some breakfast in the café?"

"Sounds like a plan." She paused, then said, "Stone . . . ?"

"What?"

She opened the car with a bleep and climbed in. I climbed in on the other side and slammed the door. She looked at me. "Why are people such assholes?"

"I don't know, partner. I was hoping you could tell me."

For the fourth time that morning we drove across the Bronx, this time toward the molten orb of the sun. Dehan spoke suddenly.

"There is only one way this makes sense. So far, nobody knows what the hell those boys were doing there at three in the morning. If Angela knows, she ain't telling; Ed, Mary, and Sue all look shocked out of their minds that their boys were there . . ."

"And, did you notice how Ed and Sue both suggested the other boy was a bad influence on their son?"

"I got that. So I'm thinking, you have two basically good,

hardworking boys who are not quite as saintly as their parents like to believe."

"Agreed."

"And, as I initially suspected, they have been taking certain medical substances from the hospital, probably fiddling the records, and selling the medication to somebody in the 'hood."

"The barrio."

"Exactly. Now, I am thinking also that maybe Angela was involved in some way, perhaps as a contact or a middleman. She was expecting them to arrive. That's why she was up and not in bed. They pull up in their car, kill the engine, but, before they can get out, somebody gets out of the car ahead of them. He doesn't need to see their faces, because he is expecting them to be there, and maybe he knows the car . . ."

"Note, we need to establish who the car belongs to."

"Agreed, noted. Stop interrupting. So our shooter is there because they are selling on his turf. He strolls over and executes them, cowboy style, empties his magazine into them and leaves."

"It's coherent and makes sense. What about the two shots in the door?"

"A previous warning."

"Hmmm . . . Okay, it's an hypothesis. Let's see what we get from Elizabeth and the hospital. We also need a list of dealers in that area who might have been mad at them for encroaching on their territory. And this afternoon, we'll grill Angela over exactly what her relationship with Sebastian and Luis was."

We lapsed into silence again, but after fifteen minutes she said to me, "I know why you're not happy."

"Yeah?"

She turned into Seminole Avenue and then headed for the parking lots.

"You're not happy because the drug-pushing theory does not allow for a connection with Rosario's murder fifteen years ago."

I nodded. "And they *are* connected, Little Grasshopper. They are connected."

"Maybe you're wrong."

I laughed.

"What? You can't be wrong?"

"They are connected."

"How?"

She pulled into a parking space, killed the engine, and turned to look at me. I stared out at the lawn, at the single plane tree with its silver peeling bark. After a moment, I shook my head and sighed.

"I don't know yet, Carmen. But I'll tell you this much. It is no coincidence that Rosario and Sebastian were killed within a few yards of each other. The house is significant. And I'll tell you something else. Luis was not the intended victim."

She frowned. "How can you know that?"

I shrugged. "Because he didn't finish him off."

She shook her head. "Nah! Seven rounds. His magazine was capped. It's the law."

"Come on, Dehan! Even if his magazine was capped. He went there for the purpose of making the kill. He didn't bring a spare magazine? All he had to do was put in a new clip, walk around the car, and finish the job. But he didn't. And he didn't because he didn't care that the passenger was getting away. His target was the driver."

She made a face. "Okay, if you say so. Let's see what Elizabeth says."

"And their other colleagues. And then please let's have breakfast."

We climbed out and headed for reception.

# FIVE

WE WERE LUCKY. WE INQUIRED IN RECEPTION AND discovered that Elizabeth Kelly was coming off duty at seven thirty that morning. So we went and had scrambled eggs and coffee and waited for her at a plastic table by a plate glass window overlooking the parking lots. She eventually walked in at ten minutes before eight, looking freshly showered but tired, in jeans and a sweatshirt. We stood as she approached and shook hands with her. She was polite but didn't look happy to meet us.

"What is this about? I'm at the end of a twelve-hour shift and I would really like to get home and sleep."

I produced a smile that looked like an apology. "I understand, can we offer you a coffee?"

"No, thank you. As I said, I'd like to get home . . ."

I gestured to a chair, and she sat reluctantly. Dehan smiled at her in a way that did not look like an apology and said, "We won't keep you any longer than is absolutely necessary, Ms. Kelly. We've slept three out of the last twenty-six, so we are pretty keen to get moving too. We just have a couple of questions. How well do you know Sebastian Acosta?"

She looked surprised. "Seb? We're pretty close. First-year residency doesn't allow you much of a personal life, but we see each other when we can. We've talked about moving in together, a future someday. Why?"

Dehan gave a small grimace. "When was the last time you saw him, Elizabeth?"

Now Elizabeth looked worried. Her eyes flicked to me and then back to Dehan. "About twelve hours ago. He was going off duty and I was coming on. Can you please tell me what this is about?"

Telling someone a loved one has died is one of the worst things you can do in life. Doing it to four people in five hours is exhausting. I drew a deep breath and said, "Elizabeth, I am really sorry to have to tell you this, but Sebastian was killed in the early hours of this morning."

It was as though she'd been slapped in the face. She went rigid, and the color drained from her already pale cheeks. Her right hand covered her mouth. At first she looked angry, like we had insulted her. Then the tragedy and the sadness flooded her eyes. She shook her head. "Not Sebastian. No . . ."

Dehan gave a small sigh. "I'm really sorry. There is no doubt about the identity."

"How . . . ? You're asking me how well I knew him. Why? What's happened?"

"He and Luis were shot at about three o'clock this morning."

She stared at us like we were insane. "*Shot?* That's ridiculous! There must be some mistake. Why would anyone . . . ?"

I shook my head. "The medical examiner identified them both."

Her head snapped around to look at me. "The ME? Frank . . ."

I nodded. "He seemed to be fond of them."

She was stoic. I guess you learn that as a doctor. But you could see the pain in her face as the inescapable nature of what had happened dawned on her. She wasn't going to wake up from this. It wasn't going to turn out to be a bad dream, a misunderstanding, or a mistake. It was real. Her eyes were resentful, turning red as they flooded with tears.

"Why?"

I repeated the morning's ongoing refrain. "That's what we want to find out."

She stared at me, then at Dehan. "You mean it wasn't a mugging?"

Dehan shook her head. "The motive isn't clear, Elizabeth. We are going to need help. Are you up to answering some questions?"

She nodded, staring at her hands in front of her on the table. "Of course. Where are they? Is Luis dead too?"

"Luis is in a bad way, but as far as we know, he is still alive. He's here. So is Sebastian."

"Elizabeth." I paused a moment, not exactly sure how to frame the question for her. "As far as you know, were Sebastian and Luis involved in anything . . ." I paused again. She was frowning at me, wondering where I was going with my question. "Anything risky or dangerous? Anything that could have made them enemies, targets for somebody?"

"Like what?"

I shrugged. "This is a hospital. You tell me . . ."

She shook her head. "No! Nothing. Of course not! He was dedicated, committed, very serious. He wouldn't have done anything stupid. Neither of them would."

Dehan leaned her elbows on the table. "Think carefully before answering, Elizabeth. It may have been something that to them seemed harmless or unimportant, but to somebody else . . ."

She left the words hanging. Elizabeth sat looking at her for a moment. Then her eyes drifted. Dehan waited, then asked, "What is it?"

She shrugged. "It may be nothing, and I don't want to get anyone into trouble . . ."

I smiled, but it must have looked sad and tired, because that was how I felt. I said, "More trouble than they are in already?"

She studied my face, then gave a sigh that shuddered. "I guess you're right. As I say, it may be nothing, but Luis . . ." She sighed again. "Luis was hanging out a lot with a girl, Lynda, she works at the pharmacy here, in the hospital."

Dehan sat back in her chair, frowning. "Okay . . ."

Elizabeth hesitated some more, uncomfortable with what she was doing. "She mentioned a few times to Luis that the pharmacist is not exactly meticulous in how he keeps his records. One night she was joking about getting some Cialis for the boys. Luis pretended to get excited about what else she could get. I didn't think it was funny. Neither did Sebastian." She sighed again, shrugged, spread her hands. "It's nothing! It's just that Seb and I never really liked her much. She's a bit wild. Luis is a bit wild too, and they kind of sparked each other off. We thought she was a bad influence on him. But I'm pretty sure he would never actually do anything.

"She's Australian. She says that back home, she has a degree in chemistry. Maybe she has, I don't know. But here she can't practice. I don't know exactly how legal her position is. Anyway, I guess it's possible that she and Luis may have been taking stuff from the pharmacy and selling it. I really don't think so, but it's *objectively* possible."

She stopped, covered her face with her hands, and shook her head. "That sounds so awful! And I have no grounds whatever to make such an accusation, other than I don't really like her much, and she's a bit crazy and out there. She's probably a perfectly decent person."

I nodded that I understood. "If there is nothing in it, they have nothing to worry about. What's her surname, do you know?"

"Graham, Lynda Graham."

"And she is Luis' girlfriend?"

She shrugged. "Kind of, not exactly. They hang out together, go out together sometimes. I know they sleep together. But it seems to be a pretty open relationship. I think there is or was another guy in her life, but I don't know anything about him."

Dehan grunted, then asked, "What do you know about Angela Rojas?"

"Angela?" Again she looked surprised at the question. "Not a lot. I met her a couple of times socially. I know she was like a half sister to Seb and Luis. Why? What's she got to do with this?"

"Can you think what they would have been doing outside her house at three in the morning?"

She stared at Dehan for a long moment, and you could tell she was seeing the scene playing itself out in her mind. "Is that where it happened?"

Dehan nodded. "Yes."

She took a deep breath and closed her eyes. After a moment, she said, "No, not really. At least, I don't know what Seb was doing there. Luis is a real party animal. I don't know where he finds the energy. He used to drag Seb along all the time, but Seb and I had talked about it, and he'd decided to pull back a bit. He couldn't afford it, for one thing, and he couldn't take the pace. The fact is we were both finding Luis and Lynda hard work."

I asked her, "How about Angela? Is she a party animal?"

She shrugged. "I don't know. She didn't strike me that way, but she might be."

"I'm sorry to have to ask this, Elizabeth, but, to the best of your knowledge, was either of the boys having an intimate relationship with her?"

She winced a bit, like I'd hurt her feelings. "No, at least, I know Sebastian wasn't. I don't know about Luis. But like I said, I think it was more like brothers and a sister. They'd known each other all their lives. They grew up together. I think their parents were friends or something."

I looked at Dehan. "I think that's all we need to know for now . . ."

Dehan said, "There is just one more thing. Sebastian was driving a Toyota Corolla . . ."

Elizabeth frowned. "A Toyota?" She shook her head. "Seb's car is an old VW Beetle. He called it his project. It's at the mechanic's right now . . . I guess that's one project he'll never finish . . ." She stopped, steadied herself, took a deep breath. "Luis drives a second- or thirdhand Ford Probe. I don't know whose Toyota that was. Maybe they borrowed it from somebody." She glanced at us each in turn. "It looks like there was a lot about them both that I didn't know . . ."

She pulled out her cell and called her mother to come and collect her. Two minutes later, we watched her walk out of the café, holding it together until she got home. Then everything would fall apart. Then she would allow the full horror, the full, inescapable reality of it to hit her. Dehan puffed out her cheeks and blew, then rubbed her face with her hands and ran her fingers through her hair. It was an eloquent combination of gestures, and it expressed pretty well how I felt myself.

"Well, Detective Stone," she said, and slapped her hand on my shoulder, "it's looking like the boys were playing fast and loose with the pharmacy, and Lynda, the pharmacist's assistant. I say we take her downtown and ask her a few tough questions, whadd'ya say, partner?"

"I say it's looking like one to Detective Dehan and nil to Detective Stone. But it's early yet. I say we make like cannibals and grill this girl."

She suppressed a laugh and shook her head. "Nice. That's nice."

As we crossed the café toward the door, in search of the pharmacy, she was still chuckling and repeating under her breath, "Make like cannibals and grill this girl . . ."

We made our way out to Pelham Parkway and found the pharmacy in building one. There was a pretty young girl behind the counter. She was in her early twenties, tall and blond, with mischievous eyes which smiled as we stepped in.

"Good morning!" She said it with that curious, antipodean singsong.

I smiled back. "Hi, we are NYPD detectives." I showed her my badge. "I am Detective Stone; this is my partner, Detective Dehan. Are you Lynda Graham?"

Her face became wary. "Ah . . . yeah . . . Why?"

Dehan gave a small, not unfriendly laugh. "Was that a yes, Lynda?"

"Yeah, I guess it was. What's the problem?"

"We need to ask you some questions about Luis Irizarry and Sebastian Acosta. We'd like you to accompany us to the station."

"Oh, shit! Look . . ." She glanced over her shoulder toward the back of the shop. I figured her boss was in there. Her voice dropped. "Me and Luis? I don't know what he's told you, but we just hang out? We're friends?" She had that Australian trick of making statements sound like questions. She looked from me to Dehan and back again. "I don't know anything, I mean, I don't know . . ."

She trailed off. We waited a moment while she stared at us. Finally, I said, "Lynda, this is a murder inquiry, and we would like you to come down to the station to answer some questions."

Her jaw literally dropped. She gaped at me. "*Murder?* Holy *shit!*"

I gave a humorless smile. "What did you think it would be, Lynda?"

"Ay? No . . . ! Nothing! I didn't . . . I don't know . . . *Murder?*"

# SIX

It was thirty minutes past nine in the morning. We'd been going for six hours after just three hours' sleep. I wasn't sure if my backache had given me a headache or if it was the other way around, but they both ached. We sat opposite Lynda in interview room three. I sipped strong black coffee and thought about organizing my thoughts.

Dehan got there first.

"When was the last time you saw Luis, Lynda?"

It occurred to me as she asked it that Lynda was still under the impression that it was Luis who had been murdered. I glanced at Dehan and realized that she was aware of this too. She held Lynda's eye while Lynda stared at her and swallowed three times without saying anything. Dehan cocked her head on one side.

"Is there a problem, Lynda?"

"No . . . um . . . I'm just thinking? Um, last night?"

Dehan frowned like she was confused. "Are you telling me or asking me, Lynda? When was the last time you saw Luis?"

"Last night."

"At what time?"

"Oh, um . . . like, eight o'clock? Maybe a bit later."

"Where did you see him?"

"Him and Seb? Come over to my place for a few beers?"

"Where, Lynda? Where is your place?"

"Victor Street. It's like White Plains and Morris Park, where they meet? Just kind of there."

"And who else was there?"

"No! I mean, nobody. I mean, you know, a friend might have dropped in . . ." She began chewing her lip. "But it was just me and the guys . . ." She grinned at me and then at Dehan.

I asked her, "Who dropped in?"

"Um, maybe Jack? I'm not sure, you know, we got pretty maggot."

"You got what?"

"Maggot, off our faces, wasted . . ."

"Drunk."

"That's the one."

Dehan put both hands palm down on the table and stared at them like she was wondering what they were doing there. "Let me see if I've got this straight, Lynda. Eight or eight thirty, Luis and Sebastian turn up at your place on Victor Street, and the three of you settle down for an evening of drinking. You all got very drunk and maybe your friend Jack paid a visit."

"Uh-huh . . ." She looked at me with her eyes, then back at Dehan.

"How long did they stay?"

"Few hours. Like I say, we got pretty mag . . . pissed, drunk."

I leaned forward on my elbows, grinned. "So you had good fun. It was a good evening."

She liked that and smiled back. "Oh, deadest!"

"So how come Jack didn't stay?"

"Um . . ." Again her eyes swiveled, first to Dehan, then back to me. "He was . . . um . . ."

I gave a small laugh and raised one hand. "Lynda, stop." She closed her mouth. "Between us, Detective Dehan and I must have over thirty years' experience doing this job, in the Bronx. How many liars do you think we have interviewed in this room over that time? If it were just two a week—and believe me, it is many more than that—that would be over three thousand. And just about every one of them was a better liar than you. You are a really *bad* liar, Lynda!" I laughed in a kindly, uncle-ish kind of way. "That's not a bad thing. That's a good thing, right?"

She nodded.

"Now, listen to me, you are probably not in trouble. If you are, it's probably not serious trouble. But keep bullshitting us and you will certainly end up in real *bad* trouble. So, quit stalling and tell the truth. You understand me?"

She looked like she understood me but wasn't necessarily convinced.

"Well, Jack doesn't really like Luis much? I mean, I am really sure that he would not do anything. I mean, I *know* he wouldn't. But like, when he saw Luis was there, he just chucked a fuckin' spaz and left."

Dehan pinched the bridge of her nose. "Chucked a spaz?"

"Yuh, fuckin' wobbly right there! I mean, who fuckin' needs it, right? I told the fuckin' dickhead to buzz off and go home."

"He got mad and you told him to leave?"

"Too right."

"And he left?"

"Yeah."

"What time would that be, Lynda? Please don't tell me you were maggot and you don't know. This is a murder inquiry. Make an effort."

She gave me a sheepish smile. I gave her a wink.

"Well, I suppose, we'd had a few grogs by then, so it would have been after ten? Maybe half ten, half eleven . . . ?"

Dehan's face was tight. "What does that mean? Half ten, half eleven . . ." She shook her head. "What does it mean?"

I smiled. "It means ten thirty or eleven thirty. Lynda, I'm having trouble with something. See if you can help me. Do you drive?"

"Back home, yeah."

"You don't own a Toyota?"

"No."

"So, if Luis and Sebastian are"—I smiled—"off their faces and totally maggot, how did they drive to Hunts Point in a Toyota Corolla?"

"I don't know, honest to God, I don't."

"Okay, Lynda. Let's talk about something else." I scratched my chin and realized I needed a shave. "How long have you and Luis been stealing drugs from the pharmacy?"

Her eyes went like saucers, the blood drained from her face, and she started shaking her head. "No! No! No way! No! Not me! You got the wrong person! I never done that! No way!"

I ignored her and pressed on. "How about Jack? Did he buy the stuff from you? Is that why he dropped in, to collect the merchandise?"

Her voice had become shrill. "*No!* Look! This is bollocks! I ain't stupid! How fuckin' stupid would I have to be to do that?"

I continued to ignore her. "How about Angela? Did she distribute the stuff in Hunts Point?"

"*Who?*"

"I told you you're a terrible liar, Lynda. Cut it out. Tell me the truth. You had a deal going, you and Luis, Jack and Angela. How much were you netting a week?"

"*Stop it!* You are *wrong*! This is *bullshit*!"

"Was Sebastian involved?"

"*No!* Look—*nobody was involved!* It just didn't happen! Check with the fuckin' pharmacy, for God's sake! There are no missing supplies!"

I nodded. "We plan to. Where can we find Jack? Has he got a surname?"

"Oh, that's fuckin' ace! He's going to love me, isn't he? Sending the fuckin' Jacks 'round!"

Dehan sighed. "Jacks?"

I smiled at her. "Jack Law, the cops. Why would he have a problem with the law coming 'round?"

She looked at me like I was crazy. "You know anyone who actually *welcomes* you when you turn up unannounced? 'Oh, hey, look! Put the kettle on, it's the fuzz!'"

"So where can we find him?"

"Look at me! Minding my own fuckin' business, I have a couple of grogs with some mates, and next thing, you're trying to frame me for drug trafficking and *fuckin'* murder!"

"Take it easy. Nobody is trying to frame you. What's his surname, and where can we find him?"

"Fuckin' *strewth*!"

Dehan spoke softly, "Lynda . . ."

Lynda stared at her.

"Jack . . . ?"

"O'Brien. Hunt Avenue, 1719 B."

"Cell phone?"

She recited it. Dehan wrote it down and said, "You'd rather we didn't tell him who gave us his name and address?"

She narrowed her eyes and spoke with something like venom, "*Oddly* enough!"

Dehan shrugged. "You cooperate with us, we'll cooperate with you."

She glanced at me, then back at Dehan. "What's that supposed to mean?"

"All we want is to find out who did this killing. We are not interested in anything else. We certainly don't want to cause unnecessary problems for you . . ."

She looked as though a black mamba had just offered her a cup of tea and a biscuit.

Dehan went on, "Jack O'Brien got a job?"

Lynda thought about this for a long time before answering. "Not that kind . . ." She sighed. "No. I don't know what he does. I've bought mull, um . . . weed from him sometimes."

Dehan bobbed her head. "So think about this really carefully, Lynda. If we check the stores and the pharmacy, and if we get a warrant to search your house and Jack's, are we going to find drugs missing at the pharmacy, and those same drugs at your house or at Jack's?"

"*No!* Fuckin' do it! *Please!*"

I drummed on the table for a moment. "So, what exactly was the relationship between you and Luis?"

She shrugged. "We were mates." Then she smiled at me. "Mates with privileges."

"How about you and Jack?"

"Same kind of thing, only he thinks it's more. He does this whole fuckin' jealous macho number on me."

Dehan frowned and gave her head a small shake. "You don't seem real broken up about what happened."

She seemed genuinely shocked by the comment. "Give me a fuckin' chance! When you stop fuckin' harassing me and trying to fuckin' frame me, when I get home and you're not fuckin' jumping down my fuckin' throat, then I'll cry my fuckin' eyes out! I fuckin' loved Luis!"

I studied her a moment and thought that perhaps she was telling the truth. People process grief in different ways. And we had seen plenty of that during the morning. I looked at Dehan. She said, "Please don't leave town, Lynda. We may need to talk to you again."

She stood up. "Fuckin' priceless!"

I leaned back in my chair. "Lynda, I think there has been a bit of a misunderstanding."

She froze, staring into my face. "What?"

"I think you've been under the impression that Luis was murdered."

She frowned, then scowled at Dehan. "You *said* . . . !"

"No, what Detective Dehan said was that this was a murder inquiry. She didn't say that Luis had been murdered. Luis was badly injured and is in critical condition in the hospital. It was Sebastian who was murdered. They were both shot, Sebastian died. Luis may yet die, but as far as we are aware, he is still alive."

"You *fuckin'* dipsticks."

She slammed out of the room and left a ringing silence behind her. Dehan stood and stretched, then walked around the room with her hands in her back pockets. She said to the wall, "What's your impression?"

I laughed quietly to myself. "Right now, I'd like to get maggot and then get some shut-eye."

She turned and smiled at me. "Two nations divided by a common language."

I nodded. "Shaw, but he was talking about us and the English. I don't know, Dehan. I don't believe she is a model, law-abiding citizen. She likes her dope and her booze. She has a house, albeit a small one, on a shop assistant's salary. So she is getting money from somewhere other than her job."

She nodded. "On the other hand, I don't get the impression she's making a stash. If she was supplying Jack and Angela, I'd expect her to be making more money than she seems to be."

I drummed the table with my palms. "This may not even be our case, Dehan. Let's go talk to the inspector, tell him what we have, and see what he thinks."

She nodded. "Okay, Sensei. Let's go."

Inspector John Newman was in his office. We knocked, and he told us to enter. When we did, he was by the window, watering a small fern on the sill. He smiled at us with what looked like genuine pleasure.

"Come in, come in. Please sit." He made his way back to his desk and lowered himself carefully into his large, black leather chair. He had tightly curled black hair going gray at the temples. That and his olive skin made him look like a villain from a Zorro movie.

"I imagine you are here about the Irizarry murder."

It was Dehan who answered. "Yes, sir. We are unclear how to proceed and we would appreciate your guidance."

I raised an eyebrow at her but remained silent, contemplating the possibility that Inspector John Newman might be the only man in the world whom Carmen Dehan had ever asked for guidance.

He nodded slowly. "You are unclear whether it is a cold case or not."

I said, "That's right, sir. Angela Rojas is clearly connected to the case—and the murder—in that she was like a sister to the two victims. Her mother, who was a close friend of the victims' parents, was murdered, fifteen years ago, in the same house outside which the boys were shot. As far as it goes, that is quite compelling. However, the details of the shooting so far do not suggest any link between the two crimes."

Inspector Newman frowned and thrust out his lower lip. Before he could say anything, Dehan spoke, "However, sir, Detective Stone has a strong hunch, or intuitive feeling . . ."

"I know what a hunch is, Detective. At one time, I also used to have them." He smiled. "I *am* a cop."

"Yes, sir. Detective Stone has a strong hunch that the two cases are, in fact, connected. And in my experience, his hunches tend to be accurate."

I added, "Or ace."

He frowned at me. "Excuse me?"

"Ace, accurate, spot-on."

"Well, you have the case, I have no doubt you will tackle it with the same genius you bring to the cold cases, and if you can find a link to Mrs. Rojas' murder and solve that too, then so much the better. Does that resolve your dilemma?"

Dehan smiled. "Yes, sir. Thank you."

"Glad I could help! If only all problems were that simple, hey?"

"That would be ripper, sir."

We stood, I opened the door for Dehan, and we left, all of us smiling at each other.

On the stairs, I asked her, "What was that?"

"What was what?"

"Detective Stone's hunches are always dinky-di."

"Enough already with the Australian slang!"

"You want this case, Dehan."

"So what if I do?"

We had arrived at the door to the detectives' room. I looked at my watch. "Here's the plan. We go and talk to Jack O'Brien, then we go and check on Luis, see how he's doing, and after that we grab some lunch and a grog."

"Again?"

"I tell you, Sheila, I am as dry as a dingo's donger!"

She sighed, shook her head, and made for her car, muttering, "*Dios!*"

# SEVEN

WE PARKED A FEW DOORS DOWN FROM HIS HOUSE. Dehan looked at me and I thought she smiled, but it wasn't clear. She said, "I got this."

I allowed my eyebrows to visit my hairline in an expression of surprise and said, "Okay . . ."

She loosened her hair, ruffled it up a bit in the mirror, undid her top two buttons, and leered at me. Then she did a fair imitation of Sylvester the cat. "Do I look thexy, Detective Thtone?"

"Irresistible."

She got out and slouched down the road with her hands in her pockets. When she got to 1719 B she stopped, looked up and down the road a couple of times, and knocked on the door. Then she stood staring down at her feet with her shoulders hunched. After a moment she looked up. I couldn't see the door, though I guessed it had opened. She spoke but wouldn't make eye contact, looked up the road, at her feet, laughed like a shy girl, then went quiet, listening, staring down at the sidewalk. She nodded a couple of times and now she made eye contact. Said something and turned to beckon me. I climbed out of the car and headed toward the house.

Next thing, there was a rush of movement. Dehan staggered back. A big guy, maybe six three, in jeans and a black T-shirt was shoving her. She stumbled against a fire hydrant and fell. Then he was running, sprinting. I shouted, "*NYPD! Freeze!*" But he was too hot to freeze.

Dehan was scrambling to her feet even before she'd hit the ground. I started to run, but she made off like an Olympic sprinter. Before I'd run four paces, she'd taken eight and she was on his heels. Next thing, she was flying in midair. She wrapped her arms around his knees, held tight, and he went down like a sack of wet sand.

By the time I got to them, she was sitting astride his back, cuffing his wrists. He was wheezing badly. She stood, grabbed him by the scruff of his neck, and dragged him to his feet.

"Sap! Detective Stone, this man offered to sell me an ounce of marijuana. When I informed him that I was a police officer, he attempted to flee."

"I saw the whole thing, Detective Dehan."

He turned to look at us. He was almost bald and had pale blue eyes and a jaw like a slab of concrete. He looked mad too. "Nah," he said, and shook his head. "You got it all wrong, incha? I weren't running. Thought I saw me mate, and went after him!"

I raised an eyebrow. "You're British."

"English, mate. It's different."

"Right, you can tell us all about it inside. Get going."

Dehan led him back to the house, a small, gray clapboard affair with a sharp, gabled roof and a wrought iron gate over the door. She shoved him inside, and we followed after him through a hallway and into a small, open-plan living room and kitchen, where I noticed a cellar door. There were two beaten-up sofas, a threadbare IKEA chair, and a TV, plus the obligatory pizza boxes and empty cans of beer. I guess you're not a real guy if you haven't got the takeout pizza boxes and the cans. He turned to face us.

"Am I under arrest?"

I made a face and danced my head around in a "maybe you are and maybe you're not" kind of way. "That depends on you. Is your name Jack O'Brien?"

"Not much point denying that, is there?"

"Not really, Jack, no."

"So how is it up to me?"

I pointed at the sofa and said, "Sit down, Jack. Let's talk."

His jaw set and his face took on a kind of obstinate, blank look. "If you ain't arresting me, Detective, I'd like you to remove my handcuffs. Then we can talk."

I glanced at Dehan; she shrugged and moved toward him. He grinned at her with what looked like genuine appreciation. "Where'd you learn to rugby tackle, then? You done all right."

She almost smiled and unlocked his cuffs. "At badass school, when I was four."

He chuckled and sat. I sat on the other sofa, and Dehan put her ass on the windowsill, by the door, with her arms crossed. I offered him an expression of wry amusement among guys.

"Here's the thing, Jack. We're not from vice."

He frowned, trying to work out where I was going.

I looked over at where the door to the basement stood in the open-plan kitchen. "Obviously, we have probable cause, Jack. So, what do you think I am going to find if I go down into your basement? How many plants am I going to find?" He opened his mouth to speak, but I tapped my nose. "I can smell it."

He closed his mouth and sighed. Dehan shook her head. "You should have gone to Colorado or Cali. New York has strict laws on dope."

He nodded at her. "But you can't get the price, can you? Everyone's fuckin' at it out there, growing their own. Make it legal and the bleedin' price goes through the floor." He looked back at me. "What do you want, then, if you're not vice?"

"What can you tell me about Luis Irizarry?"

He frowned a moment, then his face cleared. "Oh, that

wanker! Luis." He shrugged. "Not a lot. Thinks he's a fuckin' cut above everybody else just 'cause he's a doctor. That, and he's got his fuckin' sights on my girl . . ."

Dehan said, "Your girl?"

"Yeah, my girlfriend, you know . . ."

"Yeah, I know what a girl is, Jack. Who is she? What's her name?"

He narrowed his pale blue eyes. "Why d'you wanna know that? What's she got to do with anything?"

I raised my eyebrows at him and tilted my head on one side. "Just answer the question, Jack. Alternatively, we can do this by the book down at the station, record the interview, get a warrant . . ."

"All right, all right. Lynda, Lynda Graham. But she ain't involved in nothing dodgy. She's a nice girl, got a proper job, nice house. I help her out with the rent a bit . . ."

I nodded. "That's good of you, Jack. So, what I hear you saying is that you are making a commitment to Lynda."

He got a faraway look in his eyes and smiled. "I suppose I am. She's the kind of girl what might make you take a look at your life, know what I mean? Think twice about the direction you're taking an' that."

"I'm glad to hear it, because, my friend, let me tell you, where you are headed right now is not anywhere you want to be, especially if you are thinking of getting serious about a woman. If you have in that basement what I think you have in that basement, you are looking at a long sentence. By the time you get out, Lynda could be married and with kids."

He became serious. "I know. I was never doing it in a big way. It's just . . ."

"Relax, I can see you're cooperating." I gave him a man-to-man, lopsided grin. "Must have made you mad to see Luis coming on to your girl, am I right?"

He sagged back into the sofa. "He's not fuckin' serious, is he?

To him it's all a big fuckin' larf. Life's one big bleedin' party. And Lynda loves a party, don't she? So she's well up for it! And I don't mind that. I ain't the bleedin' jealous type. But she don't realize he only wants her for one thing. Me, I'm in for the long haul, ain't I? I want a commitment."

"When was the last time you saw Luis, Jack?"

"Last night. Why?"

"Where was that?"

"It's what I'm tellin' you. I went 'round to Lynda's place. She only lives 'round the corner, I knocks on the door, and I can hear fuckin' music and laughing inside. I go in and there's fuckin' Luis and a mate of his, sitting there drinking beer with my girl, in the house what I'm paying the rent for . . ."

"Must have made you pretty crazy."

He shrugged. "Well, you know, there's a fuckin' limit, ain't there?"

"So what did you do?"

"I told her, her and me needed to have a serious talk, 'cause I ain't payin' the rent on her bleedin' house so she can entertain gentlemen there. I mean, I ain't fuckin' stupid. So she has to decide whether she is serious or not." He frowned. "Here, what's this about? You didn't come here to play fuckin' agony aunt to me, did you?"

I smiled. "Not really, Jack. We're almost done. Just tell me where you went and what you did after you left Lynda's house."

"I come home, got a takeaway pizza, and watched a movie." His frown deepened. "Why? I've played straight with you guys, I have a right to know what you're questioning me about."

Dehan said, "Where were you between two and three a.m. last night?"

Now he looked alarmed. "I was here, on my couch, asleep. And I ain't sayin' another word till you tell me what this is about."

"So you have no one who can vouch for you . . ."

"I ain't got a fuckin' alibi, if that's what you're askin'. But I didn't fuckin' know I'd need one. I played fair and square with you an' you led me into a fuckin' trap! That ain't right!"

"Luis was shot last night."

"Oh, fuckin' 'ell!"

I said, "Do you own a gun, Jack?"

He turned on me. "No, of course I don't own a fuckin' gun! I ain't a fuckin' Yank, am I?" He stopped himself, closed his eyes, and took a deep breath. "Sorry, I didn't mean that the way it sounded. It's just I'm . . . You're scaring the livin' fuckin' daylights out of me. You know, we just don't go around shootin' everybody the way you do!"

I heard Dehan snort and looked at her. She was suppressing a smile. Jack shrugged. "Well, you do a bit, don't you?"

"So your defense is, 'I didn't shoot him because I am British, and we don't do that kind of thing'?"

"English. And no, that isn't my defense. Am I under arrest? Do I *need* a defense? So far, your case against me seems to be that I'm in love with a girl and Luis was flirting with her. You wanna do me for sellin' weed, that's a fair cop. But if you want to stitch me up for a murder . . ." He shook his head. "No way, mate."

I studied his face a moment. "Who said it was a murder?"

He laughed. "Come off it! You did. You said he was shot."

I sighed. "He was shot, he wasn't killed. He's in the hospital."

He shrugged again. "Well, how the fuck was I supposed to know that?"

I stood and stared down at him for a moment, trying to make up my mind what I thought about him. Finally, I said, "What else do you sell, Jack?"

He frowned. "What do you mean, crack? That kind of shit?" I nodded and he shook his head. There was fear in his eyes, more fear than I would have expected. "Oh, no, mate. No way. Not me. I sell a bit of weed to cover expenses. I don't want nuffink to do with that hard shit. Never mind what *you'd* do to me if you caught me, it's what the hard nuts 'round here would do to me. I been warned. I don't wanna know, mate. I ain't treadin' on nobody's toes. Not no way." He stood up and laughed like I was crazy. "I'm not a fuckin' criminal, mate! It's New York, you're twenty years behind the times! Anywhere else in the world, what I do would be legal! Almost."

Dehan stepped over to him and stared up into his big face. "Here it's illegal. That makes you a criminal. Get this clear, O'Brien, if vice come knocking on your door, make damn sure they find a clean house. Those boys don't mess around. You got me?" Then she hesitated and frowned. "And, Jack, if you think the gangs here are cool with you growing and selling dope, you're wrong, very wrong."

He nodded. As I reached for the door, he said, "Thanks . . ."

I said, "Don't go anywhere. We may need to talk to you again."

We stepped into the early June sun and closed the iron gate behind us. The car bleeped and flashed, and Dehan went and opened the door. I strolled after her slowly, with my hands in my pockets, chewing my lip and kicking small stones out of my path. She watched me a moment then climbed in, and I got in beside her. She fired up the engine, and as she pulled away, she said, "He's not as 'straight up' and innocent as he makes out. Or as stupid."

"I know."

"He's clever and manipulative."

"I know . . ."

"And his version of events does not square up with Lynda's."

"I know."

"Stop saying 'I know.'"

"Okay."

"Okay, so shoot my theory down in flames."

I shook my head and played the drum solo from "In-A-Gadda-Da-Vida" on my knees. "Nope."

She frowned as she turned onto Morris Park Avenue. "Why?"

I shook my head. "It is far too complicated for that. Something is wrong, and I just can't see what it is. There is something . . ." I paused and stared out the window as the houses and the shops and the trees flowed steadily past. "There is something," I said again, "*unnatural* about this murder."

"*Unnatural?*"

"I know," I said to the window. "That's what I thought."

# EIGHT

WE STOPPED FIRST AT THE VAN ETTEN BUILDING ON the hospital campus to have a talk with Frank, the ME. We found him in the morgue with Sebastian Acosta. He looked up as we came in, then nodded a few times as though we'd said something he agreed with.

"Hello, Frank."

"No surprises," he said. "He died of the head wounds. He bled profusely from the first three shots to his arm and chest. The panic would have caused an accelerated heart rate, which in turn would have increased the loss of blood. The last two shots were to his head, and those were the ones that killed him."

We approached the table and looked down at Sebastian. He looked peaceful. His panic was over. Without thinking, I muttered, "Fear no more the lightning flash, nor the all-dreaded thunder-stone."

Frank considered me a moment, then said, a little sourly, "Very appropriate. I've sent the slugs to ballistics and asked them as a personal favor to fast-track them. We're not supposed to do that, but we do. Off the record, I can tell you that in Mort's opinion . . ."

Dehan frowned. "Mort?"

"In ballistics. The holes in the door were made by a forty-five. These were a thirty-eight." He sighed. "There's something else. The first impression, when you see the car—it looks like a gangland shooting, a hit, what they used to call a cowboy."

Dehan nodded. "That was my impression."

He shook his head. "But I am pretty sure it was not. In a hit of that sort, at point-blank range, you tend to have a grouping of shots around the vital areas, head and heart. Even without thinking about it, somebody who is used to using a gun points it where they want the bullet to go. But here . . ." He shook his head again. "Especially if you factor in the two shots that hit Luis, those rounds were flying all over the place. You have one in the upper arm, one through the sternum, and one in the lower left lung, then one in the temple and the other through the back of the cranium. Meanwhile, two have missed Sebastian completely and hit Luis, one in the lower left lung, and the other in the left shoulder. The shots were erratic, and that means something . . ."

Dehan said what it meant: "He wasn't used to using a gun. The recoil was making it jump. And it's only a thirty-eight . . ."

Frank nodded at her. "Exactly. Whoever shot these boys was not used to using a gun."

Dehan gave me her "told you so" face. I ignored it and asked Frank, "Any news on Luis?"

His answer was dry, carefully unemotional. "He's in a coma. He lost a lot of blood." He hesitated a moment, frowning down at Sebastian. "I have taken this very personally, John. I liked these boys, they were friends. I had high hopes for both of them, but especially Sebastian. He was a very committed young man, he should have had a full and rewarding life. Instead, this . . ." He gestured at the corpse on the table. "This senseless act has robbed him of everything, and robbed the world of a fine human being. And there aren't many of those."

"I hear you."

"Anything you need on this one, I'll put in the extra hours on my own time if need be."

I thought for a moment. "How well did you know them, Frank?"

He shrugged. "We didn't hang out together, obviously. I am twice their age, but they sometimes joined me for lunch. We talked a lot. Sebastian asked my advice on his career choice. We had a good rapport. I think I knew them quite well. Why?"

I put it to him straight. "You think Luis was the type to steal drugs from the hospital and sell them?"

He frowned hard at me, then sat slowly on one of his bench stools. "You think they might have been there selling? They strayed into somebody's territory and got punished?"

Dehan shrugged. "It's all we've got at the moment."

He thought about it a long time, then shook his head. "No." Then he shrugged. "Obviously, you have to go with the evidence, but off the record, my personal opinion is that Luis would not do that. He is a very ethical, moral young man. A ladies' man, a flirt, a party animal, certainly all that, but fundamentally a very moral, ethical young man. And Sebastian even more so. I would be truly astonished if that turns out to be the cause of this killing."

I stared at Dehan a moment and she stared back at me. Finally, I said, "Okay, thanks, Frank. We'll keep you posted."

"Please do."

We stepped out into the sunshine and walked slowly through the gardens toward the main hospital complex. Dehan watched her feet, with her hands in her pockets, and I stared at the trees, without seeing them. Eventually, she stopped and spoke without looking at me.

"If we are wrong about the motive, and it seems we might be, what possible reason could anybody have to ambush these two boys and kill them?"

I turned to face her and sighed. I held up two fingers. "Two more important points: How did the killer know they were going to be there? And, increasingly, it is looking as though Sebastian was the intended victim."

She nodded for a bit, gazing at the grass, like the grass was slowly beginning to make sense. "We really need to find out who owns that Toyota." She started to walk again and I fell in beside her. "One minute, Stone, they are having a party with Lynda; next minute, they are parked outside Angela's house, in somebody else's car, and they are ambushed."

"I agree. Whose car is it? What made them use that car? And what was their purpose in being outside Angela's house at three a.m.?"

We entered the hospital, and at the reception desk, I showed the receptionist my badge and asked where Luis Irizarry was. She checked her computer and gave me the directions to his room.

When we found it, I peered through the glass panel in the door and saw Ed standing with his back to me, talking to a large man in a white coat. Between them, I could see Mary's small, worried face. Luis was in the bed, intubated and motionless, connected to a heart monitor. I knocked and we pushed in. Ed and the doctor turned to look at us.

The doctor frowned. "Who are you?"

Simultaneously, Ed said, "What do you want?"

I ignored him and nodded to Mary. "Mrs. Irizarry." I showed the doctor my badge. "Doctor, I'm Detective Stone, and this is my partner, Detective Dehan. We are investigating this shooting. We were at the ME's office and thought we'd check on Luis and see how he was. Do you mind if I ask what his prognosis is?"

Ed spoke before the doctor could draw breath. "Dr. Delgado, you will answer no questions from these detectives! My son's records are covered by . . ."

Dr. Delgado had a big voice to go with his big body, and he used it now to good effect. "Mr. Irizarry, I am well aware of my obligations to my patients."

Ed's mouth snapped shut.

Delgado turned to me and added, "And to the police. Luis is scheduled for surgery this afternoon. He is in a coma at the moment. It is very hard to make a prognosis until we have removed the bullets and patched him up." He smiled comfortably at his own reassuringly colloquial usage. "If you would like to give me a contact number, I'll have somebody call you as soon as there is any kind of development."

I gave him my card, and he excused himself and left. As soon as the door closed behind him, Ed was snarling again. "What are you doing here, Detective? Why aren't you out there looking for whoever did this to my son?"

I raised an eyebrow at him. "Well, if you would like to tell me exactly where 'out there' is, I will gladly go there and look for him."

He screwed up his forehead and said, "Eh?"

I sighed. "We are 'out there' looking for the man who did this to your son, Mr. Irizarry. 'Out there' happens to be in here right now." I pointed in the general direction of Frank's office and said, "The medical examiner, and here, to know whether we are dealing with a double homicide or, if not, what Luis can tell us about what happened that night."

His lips clenched into a tight line. "No. Oh, no. No way."

Dehan gave a small, incredulous laugh. "Excuse me?"

"I know cops, and there is no way you are talking to my son. No way. You talk to me; I am his attorney."

I frowned. "Does he need an attorney, Mr. Irizarry?"

He glared at me. "*Anyone* who talks to the cops needs an attorney! You talk to my son and before you know it, you'll have him framed for that little skunk's murder!"

Dehan crossed her arms and raised an eyebrow. "Skunk, Mr. Irizarry?"

He advanced a step toward her, stabbing at her with a fat, hairy finger. "I know you, Detective Dehan, clawed your way out of the gutter, stepping on friends and family along the way, watching them get abused, framed, and exploited by your new friends and colleagues, the *pigs* you call police officers. I know you, I know all of you, and you will not get your claws into my son!"

She didn't move, but I saw her cheeks flush. When she spoke, her voice was quiet and steady. "You'd better watch that finger,

Counselor; if it gets any closer to my chest, we're going to have a problem."

He scowled at her and withdrew his hand.

I said, "That's the second time you have made reference to Sebastian in that way. What makes you call him a skunk?"

He laughed out loud. It was an ugly noise. "Oh! So now you're going to slander the dead boy? Of course! A white med student gets shot in the Bronx and it's the filthy Puerto Rican gangs, the lawless Latinos! But a Puerto Rican med student gets shot and it's his *own damned fault!*"

For a moment, I had brain-ache. I frowned and shook my head. "Mr. Irizarry, it was *you* who called him a skunk. I asked you *why* you called him a skunk."

He wagged his finger at me in the negative. I looked at Mary.

She sighed. "My husband believes that Sebastian was leading Luis astray . . ."

Ed turned on her. "Don't you dare feed them ammunition! Do you know what these people are capable of doing with a state-ment like that?" He turned and pointed his finger at me. "That was hearsay! It is not admissible, and what is more, I deny it!"

Dehan sighed heavily. "Mr. Irizarry. You cannot have it all ways. We want to catch the person who shot Luis, but if you obstruct us at every turn, you are going to make that very difficult to do."

He curled his lip. "That's right, blame your own inadequacies on us!"

I shook my head. "Don't use the plural, Mr. Irizarry. Your wife wants to help find the man who murdered Sebastian and attempted to murder your son. It is only you who seem hell-bent on stopping us, and frankly, I am beginning to wonder why."

His face went crimson. "*Take your threats and get the hell out of here! Get out!*"

I took a step closer to him, so we were barely inches apart, and looked at Mary. "Mrs. Irizarry, Mary, I hope your son makes a full recovery. When he does, I trust that you will prevail upon him to talk to us and tell us everything he knows." I looked down at Ed's scarlet, trembling face, and added, "It is possible that whoever tried to kill him may try again." I looked back at Mary. "It is important that we get every bit of help we can to catch this killer. Thank you, Mrs. Irizarry."

I moved to the door and pulled it open, and Dehan stepped out, but before I did, I turned to Ed. "I hope, Ed, that you will change your mind and decide to tell me exactly what it was that you had against Sebastian."

I waited a moment, but he just stared and trembled. So I shrugged and stepped out after Dehan.

We rode down in the elevator in silence, crossed the big, echoing, tiled lobby, and stepped into the bright, midday sun. Then we walked in silence back toward the Van Etten Building and her car. As we climbed in, I asked her, "You about ready for lunch?"

She nodded. "Yeah. You want to grab some beef sandwiches while I trace the Toyota?"

I was a little surprised but didn't show it. It had become almost a habit for us to grab a pizza or a burger at lunchtime, with a quick beer and a review of the case. I said, "Sounds like a plan," and she pulled away without answering.

# NINE

SHE DROPPED ME AT THE CORNER, AND I STEPPED INTO the deli to get two beef sandwiches. The bell clanked unsonorously overhead, the door clunked closed, and my senses were invaded by the aroma of freshly baked bread, smoked ham, and spices. Larry was leaning on the counter with his huge forearms and an amused glint in his eye.

"What can I do for you, Mr. Stone?"

"Hi, Larry. Give me two beef sandwiches, will you?"

"With extra mustard for the lady, huh?"

"Yup."

He started slicing meat on a lethal-looking machine. "So . . ." He winked at me. "How was the holiday?"

I feigned innocent ignorance. "Huh?"

He stepped back in incredulity, shrugged, and spread his arms the way only Italians know how. "What? You ain't been on holiday in seven years! You been back three days and you don't remember the holiday?"

"Oh, you mean Goa."

"Of course I mean Goa! You been anywhere else? Goa! Course I mean Goa!" He started cutting again. "So, come on, spill, how was it?" He nodded and winked. "Good? Huh? Everything good?"

"Yeah. It was good, great. Nice to get away."

He stared at me, winced, and shook his head. "Ahhh, *porca miseria*! You struck out, huh?"

I gave him a "seriously?" look. "Don't you get enough excitement on TV, Larry?"

"Hey, we care about you, man! We rootin' for you! You make a handsome couple!"

"She's my partner. We're good friends. Now cut it out, will you!"

He shook his head, said something in Italian that sounded vaguely offensive, and handed me the two sandwiches. I carried them up Fteley Avenue toward the station house, trying to focus my mind on Luis and Sebastian, and wondering how significant Ed's behavior was. As I stepped through the door, Maria was on the desk. She jerked her head at me.

"Hey, handsome."

"Hello, beautiful."

She glanced up and down. The place was almost empty. She said, "C'mere."

I stepped over. She leaned forward on the desk and half whispered, "I been meanin' to ask you since you got back, how'd it go?"

I frowned. "How did what go, Maria?"

She grinned. "How'd it go in Goa? You know . . . 'go in Goa'?" She waggled her eyebrows.

I sighed. "Really?"

"C'mon! You can tell me! Did you . . . ? You know!" She leered.

"Mind your own business! And also no, of course not!" I pointed at her. "And don't you start spreading gossip or I will have your hide!"

She gave me a look that could only be described as compassionate. "You struck out. What *happened?*" She glanced around again, then leaned forward and whispered again, "Well you're doing *something* wrong, John! Because that girl *likes* you! And I do mean *like*!"

I pointed at her and made a warning face. She sighed, and I went into the detectives' room, pretending I was not aware of all the surreptitious glances I was receiving. I dropped Dehan's sandwich on the desk and lowered myself into my chair. She stared at me, eyes slightly narrowed, as I unwrapped my sandwich.

"Get this. The Toyota—just hazard a guess who it's registered to . . ."

I shrugged and bit into the sandwich. As I chewed, I spoke with my mouth full. "I always assumed it was Angela's."

The smile faded from her face. "Son of a bitch! How could you *assume* that?"

I shrugged again and swallowed. "It didn't make much sense that they were arriving at that time. It made more sense that they were leaving. I figured maybe they went there from Lynda's. So the odds were good that they were borrowing her car to go home."

She nodded a few times, then smiled and shook her head. "You're right."

"Still doesn't get us very far."

"But it will give us a little more leverage when we talk to her this afternoon."

"That it will."

She grabbed her sandwich and started to unwrap it. She took a big bite and leaned back in her chair to chew. We both sat like that, chewing and staring at each other. After a moment, Mo, at the desk across the aisle from ours, looked over.

"Do you know how *weird* that is? It's . . . *unsettling*!"

Dehan grinned at me and I chuckled. She looked over at Mo, who had turned back to whatever it was he was doing. "It's a Zen technique. It helps to focus the mind, right, Stone?"

I nodded. "Mm-hm . . ."

"It's from the Sacha Naso school of meditation. You should try it with Gus."

He stared at her with his mouth slightly open for a moment, then sighed and returned to his work.

I stuffed the last piece of sandwich in my mouth, screwed up the paper, and threw it in my trash can. "I want to talk to Sue again. I want to know what goes on between her and the Irizarrys. She made some quip about Luis holding Sebastian back, remember? And Ed has an obvious problem with Sebastian. We need to know what goes on there. After that, I want to talk to Angela, if she's up to seeing us. She lied about why the boys were there, and failed to mention she lent them her car. I want to know why."

Dehan looked at her watch. "If she took a pill, she's probably still out for the count."

"Okay, let's go talk to Sue again. And if Peggy the Dragon is there, you have my permission to perform a rugby tackle on her."

She stood and smiled. "That will be my pleasure, Sensei."

Mo looked at me like I was a six-month-old lettuce he'd just found in his fridge. "*Sensei . . . ?*"

I put my hand on his shoulder and smiled with real humanity and compassion. "If you feel lost, you too can come to me, Mo, and I will show you the way of the inner axolotl, the path of Sacha Naso."

"Take a hike, Stone!"

"Be at peace, Mo." I patted his shoulder and left.

In the car, as I climbed in, I said, "Sacha Naso?"

She suppressed a smile, backed out of the lot, and pulled away. Then, with the worst kind of Hollywood Chinese accent, she said, "Detective Mo, he such an asshole!"

———

AT THREE P.M., we stood on the steps outside Sue Mackenzie's house, ringing her bell again. She eventually came to the door after about five minutes, looking groggy. Her clothes were rumpled and slightly askew, like she'd been sleeping dressed. She saw who we were and opened the iron gate to us without saying anything, then led the way indoors. I saw there was a blanket on the sofa. She moved toward it, then stopped and ran her fingers through her hair.

"You want tea, coffee?"

I was about to say we didn't, but Dehan said, "You want me to make it?"

Sue nodded. "Yeah, tea." She pointed vaguely. "It's in the cupboard."

Dehan went to the kitchen and we sat. Sue curled up in the corner of the sofa and pulled the blanket up around her.

"You feel up to talking, Sue?"

She nodded.

I thought for a moment, then asked, "What's the deal with you and Ed?"

She didn't answer for a bit, then said, "What do you mean, 'the deal'?"

"When we spoke to you this morning, you said Luis was a bad influence on Sebastian. When we spoke to Ed and Mary Irizarry, Ed said that Sebastian was a bad influence on Luis." I spread my hands. "You were all real close. Then when they moved to Morris Park, you lost touch. Mary speaks kindly of you. He doesn't. It doesn't take a genius to see that you two have some kind of issue."

She spent a while picking absently at the threads in the blanket. Then she took a deep, shuddering breath. "Luis is a nice kid. He's just a bit wild. When they were younger, he was lovely to have around." She gave a wet smile. "He was always joking, always laughing. His humor was irrepressible. Sebastian loved him like a brother. Maybe if he'd had a brother . . . But Matt died . . .

"As they got older, they both proved to be very bright. But Sebastian was more than bright. He was highly intelligent, like his father. He had Matt's temperament too: dedicated, serious, kind. Luis was out to enjoy life. I always felt he was a distraction for

Sebastian. Sebastian told me I was wrong. He welcomed the distraction . . ."

Dehan came and placed two mugs of tea on the table, and handed one to Sue. She sat and noted, "From what Frank, the ME, says, Sebastian was doing very well."

"He was."

I smiled. "So Luis wasn't having that much of a negative effect."

"I guess not." She shrugged. "Mothers . . ."

I waited a moment, but she wasn't going to say any more, so I pressed the point. "Your explanation only tells half the story, Sue. It doesn't explain why Ed is so hostile."

She gave another small shrug. "Ed is hostile to everybody and everything."

"He wasn't always, though, was he? There was a time when you were all close friends."

She held the mug in both hands, staring into it as though she was trying to draw strength from the hot brew. After a moment, she said, "Do we have to do this?"

"We won't know until you tell us what it's about. For my part, Sue, I don't intend to leave a single stone unturned in my search for whoever did this."

She closed her eyes for a long moment, then opened them again. They were swollen. She looked doped, but doped with pain.

"Matt and Ed had met at college. They were both law majors, both left-wing liberals, both deeply concerned about social justice and civil rights. But Matt lacked that aggression, that killer instinct you needed to be a good defense attorney. Besides, he was always more concerned about educating people to understand and embrace equality and diversity, rather than dividing society into stereotypical good guys and bad guys, and then punishing the bad guys." She gave a small, sad laugh. "I used to tease him that he only married me as a political statement, but that wasn't true. He was the most honest, noble man I ever knew."

She paused. After a moment, Dehan asked her, "How did Ed feel about your marriage?"

Sue made a face. "To begin with, we all got on well. We all shared the same beliefs and ideals. I guess, while we were students, and just after we started work, we all felt we were making a statement with our friendship. But when Matt got ill, and we learned that there was nothing the doctors could do about it, things began to change."

"In what way?"

"The real bond of friendship had always been between Ed and Matt. Mary and I were fond of each other, but I guess the driving force of the group had always been Ed. He was very virile and strong. And he had chosen Matt for his friend. When he learned that Matt was dying, I think it hit him harder than he was willing to admit. He became increasingly aggressive, bitter, patronizing . . ."

I frowned. "Toward whom, Sue? Aggressive and patronizing toward whom?"

She was quiet for a long moment. "Toward everybody. Toward Mary, toward me . . . Then, he suddenly announced that they were moving. He was doing very well in his practice. He was popular with the Latino community, he was an active campaigner for civil rights, he was very vocal, and all of that added up to a thriving practice. So he announced to us that he was buying a house in Morris Park. Shortly after that, Matt died, and they moved."

Dehan was watching her with a furrowed brow, aware, as I was, that she was talking around something. She sipped her tea, waited a moment, but Sue seemed to have come to a stop. So Dehan asked the question I had been thinking.

"Sue, none of this explains Ed's hostility toward you and Sebastian."

She started to talk two or three times, but each time ended with a deep sigh. Finally, she said, "You have to understand that I was very fond of Ed, in spite of his brash character. But Ed hates me, and he hated Sebastian, because he made a pass at me and I rejected him . . . and he raped me."

# TEN

THE ROOM WAS VERY QUIET. SUE WAS STARING INTO her mug of tea, and Dehan and I were watching her closely. My mind was racing, trying to fit this new fact into the incomplete picture I had. Dehan leaned forward and placed her mug on the table and her elbows on her knees.

"Eduardo Irizarry raped you?"

"Right here, in this room. The day after my husband's funeral."

"The day *after . . . ?*"

"He'd taken to coming around during Matt's illness, ostensibly to see how I was, how I was coping. I suppose I should have said something, but to be honest, I had enough on my plate with Matt's illness, knowing I was losing him, without the added anxiety of falling out with Ed and Mary." She sighed. "Besides, he never did anything. He was always kind and thoughtful. I suppose in some way I was grateful to him for the attention. I did say a few times that it would be nice if Mary came with him, but he always made some excuse."

She went quiet, picking at the minute hairs on the blanket with her left hand. She drained her mug and set it down on the floor beside her, then spoke almost like an automaton.

"You can imagine the state I was in the day after the funeral. My doctor had given me tablets to help me sleep, and I am pretty sure I overdosed on them that night. I slept right through the morning and finally woke up when Ed rang on the bell. I came down, I must have looked a wreck. He made me some tea, and, I don't remember how it went exactly, but he started talking about how I was going to need help. Now, without Matt, without his income, alone with a small boy, how was I going to cope?" She gave a small, humorless laugh. "I could hardly believe my ears. I told him I had just buried my husband, I was doped out of my head, and I had only just got up . . . !" She spread her hands and shook her head, made eye contact with Dehan for the first time. "Couldn't it wait? But he insisted."

"He was setting the ground."

Sue nodded. "Exactly, but I was too doped up to see it. Finally, he came straight out with it. We could reach an arrangement. He could help me. They were moving, but his office is right near here, in Colgate Avenue. I could work part time, cook him lunch, sometimes he could stay the night. His wife need never know. He had it all worked out, the way men do." She looked at me and sighed. "Sorry. No offense." She turned back to Dehan, shook her head, and started to cry, picking at the threads of her blanket again.

"It was like he'd kicked me in the stomach, slapped me in the face. I couldn't believe it. I screamed at him to get out. It was the worst thing I could have done. He went crazy, called me a filthy whore, slapped me, then threw me on the sofa and raped me."

She gripped her mouth with her hand, trying to stifle the sobs. She spoke with her eyes closed and her voice muffled. "I was so scared. He gripped my throat with both hands and squeezed. I thought he was going to choke me. He was like an animal. I really thought I was going to die." She stopped, was quiet for a while, then went on, "When he left, he called me a *puta*, said that if I reported him he would destroy me."

Dehan shook her head. "Why didn't you report him, Sue?"

She spread her hands again, shook her head. It was a pathetic gesture. "I was broken. I loved my husband so much. I had lost him. I didn't know how I was going to cope with life. I was worried sick about Sebastian, about what would become of him. Can you imagine what he would have done to me in court? I was so weak, so exhausted, so *tired* . . ." Again she shook her head. "I just couldn't face it. It was easier to pretend it had never happened."

I said, "It must have been hard to see Mary after that."

"I didn't. I never saw her again. They moved a couple of months later."

She fell silent. I said absently, "But the boys stayed in touch . . ."

She nodded at the blanket. "Social media at first. Then when Luis got older, he used to come and visit . . . always against his father's wishes. I believe most of the time, he didn't know where his son was. Later, they deliberately chose to study medicine together."

There were a couple of questions burning in my mind, but something told me to wait. I glanced at Dehan, wondering if she was thinking the same. My gut told me she was. She looked at me. I gave a small nod, and she said, "I think we're done for today, Sue. You want me to call Peggy for you, tell her you're awake?"

She shook her head. "I'll call her. Thanks." Then she looked up at Dehan. "Detective . . . Carmen. May I call you Carmen? I remember you. You were older than the other kids, but I remember you." She frowned and for a moment I thought she was going to start crying again. "I've never told anybody what happened that day. It has been a real relief to get it out. Thank you."

She reached up and took Dehan's hand. Dehan gave it a squeeze. "Sure. If you need anything, you know where to find us. Just give us a call."

We let ourselves out. The sky was still bright, but you could feel the summer evening creeping in at the edges. I felt suddenly weary and leaned on the roof of the car.

Dehan leaned opposite, with the key in her hand. "Quite a day, huh?"

I nodded and glanced at my watch. "It's almost six o'clock. We've been on the go since before three. What do you say we let Angela sleep, head back to my place, and have an early supper?"

She opened the car door. "I'll drive you back, but I won't stay." She climbed in, and I climbed in after her. She fired up the engine and pulled away. "It's been a real long day, I could use some sleep."

"Sure. Me too."

We drove in a silence that started to become awkward. Eventually, I said, "So did you notice anything absent from Sue's narrative?"

She frowned. "Like what?"

"Same thing that was absent from Ed's narrative." I looked at her.

She glanced back and gave her head a quick shake. "What?"

I gave a small shrug. "Rosario."

Her frown deepened. After a moment, she said, "Huh!" and then, "I guess you're right."

"She was part of the gang. So much so that your mother stopped hanging out with her. Yet nobody talks about her. The only person who mentioned her was Mary, and that was to say that she was dead, after *we* had mentioned her. If you didn't know already that Rosario was part of that crowd, to hear them talk, you would never guess." I shrugged again. "It makes you wonder, what is it about Rosario that makes people *not* talk about her?"

She glanced at me. "Rape?"

I raised my eyebrows and sucked my teeth. "We now have two rapes in one small group of friends. To be more precise, we have three women and two rapes. And the boy who was murdered is the son of one of the rape victims."

"Yeah, that had struck me. It doesn't give us a motive, but it sure as hell suggests there might be one in there somewhere." She wagged a finger in my direction without looking at me. "I'll tell you something else. Ed is very reluctant to cooperate with the investigation. Why would a father be reluctant to cooperate with the police in investigating his own son's attempted murder?"

I stared out the window and said, absently, half to myself, "What would make him reluctant . . . ?"

"Yeah, okay, that."

"You think Ed shot his own son?"

"We already agreed visibility was terrible. He may not have known the passenger was Luis. Like you said, he didn't go and finish him off. His intended victim was the driver."

"Mm-hm . . . You have a point. But we are still left with the question, what is his motive? After all these years."

She thought for a moment. "What if Sebastian had found out about his mother's rape? Maybe he was threatening to report him."

I made an "am not convinced" face. "Rape is almost impossible to prove if you don't get forensic evidence almost immediately. There is practically nothing Sebastian could have done. Also . . ." I shook my head. "We still have that billion-dollar question—how did the killer know that they were going to be there at that time?"

She screwed up her brow. "Yeah, especially when you consider it was Angela's car, not theirs."

I closed my eyes. "They go from work to Lynda's house. They get maggot. Somehow, in the early hours of the morning, they go to Angela's. What happens there, we don't know, but they end up borrowing her car. And somehow, between their leaving Lynda and getting into Angela's car, the killer discovers where they are and decides to strike." I puffed out my cheeks and blew. "That's not a statement of fact, just an hypothesis."

"*An* hypothesis?"

"Yes. And not a very persuasive one."

"Okay. I don't see how it can be any other way." I didn't answer, and she looked at me. "Do you?"

"I'm not sure. I'm going to eat a bison steak and drink my half of a bottle of wine and think about it."

She went quiet. After a moment, she said, "You have bison steak? How?"

I smiled. "You can order it online. I thought I'd surprise you."

"That's sweet."

"I have my sweet side."

She smiled but didn't say anything, and we drove on in silence. When we pulled into Haight Avenue and she stopped in front of my house, she said suddenly, "You have. A surprisingly sweet side. Sweeter than I expected."

Somehow, she made it sound like that wasn't a good thing. I stared at her for a long moment, then asked, "Dehan, did I do anything while we were in Goa? Anything to . . ." I shrugged. "To upset you?"

She stared back at me. Her expression was hard to fathom. There was a thin smile, but that was only on her lips. Her eyes were hard and lingered somewhere between amusement and anger.

"As far as I remember, Stone, you didn't do *anything* in Goa."

I frowned.

She looked at her watch. "I'd better get going. I'm wrecked. I'll see you tomorrow."

I opened the door, hesitated, and said, "I'll pick you up in the morning."

"Enjoy your steak and your wine."

I climbed out of the car and watched her drive away into the gathering dusk with a strange feeling of unhappiness, made worse by the lack of sleep. All in all, it had been a bad day. One of those really bad days.

I went inside, slung a pizza in the oven, and cracked a cold beer.

# ELEVEN

I was woken up by my doorbell ringing. It was already light outside. I fumbled for my watch and saw it was seven a.m. I had slept little and badly. I opened the window and leaned out. First I saw Dehan's car. Then I saw her looking up at me. She gave me that inscrutable smile and said, "Put some clothes on, you'll scare the neighbors."

I said, "You have a key. Use it."

"I left it at home."

"Why?"

She shrugged. "You want to come down and open the door?"

I pulled my pants on, and a shirt, and went down to let her in. As she stepped over the threshold, she said, "I thought you'd be up."

"Yeah. I didn't sleep so well. I'm going to jump in the shower. You know where the kitchen is."

I stood for ten minutes, letting the alternating piping hot and excruciatingly cold water batter some sense into me, toweled myself dry, dressed, and went down. I stopped at the bottom of the stairs. She was standing, watching me. She still had her jacket on and her hands in her jacket pockets. There was no coffee, no bacon, no eggs. I frowned.

"What's going on?"

She did her inscrutable thing. "You ready?"

"Do you mind if I have breakfast?"

"Sure."

I went into the kitchen feeling mad and not sure why. I grabbed the percolator.

"You want coffee?"

"No thanks. I had some already."

I dropped the percolator by the sink, muttered, "Ah, forget it," and went to grab my jacket. "Let's go."

At the door, I turned back and grabbed my car keys from the dish on the breakfast bar. As I closed the door, she looked at me like she was questioning my IQ. "What're you doing?"

"Today I'm using my car. You're welcome to ride along. If you prefer to use your car, that's fine. We can communicate by radio, or cell phone."

My car is a burgundy 1964 Jaguar Mark II, and one of the few possessions I have that I am genuinely attached to. I like driving it, and it helps me to think. I climbed in and pulled the door closed. I inserted the key in the ignition and counted slowly to three. I hadn't heard the bleep of Dehan's Focus, so I figured she was going to ride with me. I turned the key as she opened the door. The engine growled, she climbed in, and I pulled away.

"Guess you should have had that coffee, huh, Stone?"

"You seemed to be in a hurry."

"Yeah. I was thinking last night about what Sue told us. It looks like the link between the two cases is rape, right?"

I nodded.

"We know from Sue that Ed raped her. There is an at least even chance that he raped and killed Rosario."

She paused, watching me, waiting for me to agree. I was feeling uncooperative and didn't say anything. So she shrugged and went on.

"I was thinking, I know you want to talk to Angela again

today, but it might be an idea if we go and talk to Rosario's sister first."

I glanced at her. "Her sister?"

"Paulina, Pauli. They were really close. They were always in and out of each other's houses. If Rosario was working some afternoon, Angela would go to Pauli's after school, they would eat at each other's homes, spend the weekend together . . . you know the kind of thing. Real close. So if Rosario was seeing somebody, or involved with a guy in any way, Pauli would know the details. I figured it might be helpful to talk to her."

I nodded. "Good call. You spoken to her?"

"Yeah, I called her last night. She's expecting us. If you're with me, she'll treat you like we're family. Just ignore her."

I frowned at her. "Thanks."

She looked embarrassed. "I didn't mean . . . I mean . . ."

"Don't worry about it, Dehan," I said sourly. "I get it. What's the address?"

"She lives on Faile Street, at the back of the gardens."

"That's the next street to Angela. They're all in walking distance, huh?"

"Yeah, family."

We got there a little after eight. It was a big, gray clapboard house with a big bow window and an ugly, white steel-tubing fence, faced in what looked like chicken wire. The rest of the street had all the signs of gentrification that were appearing all over the Bronx, but they hadn't reached this house yet. Dehan spoke half to herself.

"She's not rich. Her parents bought it. It was cheap back then. Even so, they struggled. Her son has the upstairs, with his wife and kids."

We got out and climbed the stairs. The door opened before we rang the bell. Pauli was cute. She was barely five feet, comfortably rotund, noisy, and loving. She squealed at Dehan and smothered her in kisses. I speak a little Spanish, but all I could get was "Ay!" The rest of it was too fast. After they had disengaged and exchanged "ays," she turned her attention on me, grabbed my cheeks, and planted two big kisses on my face, telling me I was very "*guapo*."

She led us inside to a big living room and I saw she had coffee and cakes that looked like French brioche laid out for us. I was grateful.

"I hope you didn't eat!" She said, "I made caw-fee and I made Mallorca! When you called last night, I thought, 'I gotta make Mallorca for Marta's little girl! Ay!" She grabbed her cheeks and squealed again. "Sit down! Sit down! How you *been*?"

We sat. Dehan was smiling. It was a nice smile, free from the sardonic twist it so often carried. "I'm good, Pauli."

She started pouring coffee. "You see your father's family much?"

"Yeah, sometimes. We stay in touch."

"Good." She said it without much conviction. Then she changed the subject. "You made detective!"

"I did."

Pauli turned to me, oozing pride like it was her own daughter. "Ain't she the best? Ain't she something special?"

It was impossible not to smile back. It was contagious. "She is that, Pauli. She is definitely special."

The coffee was good. The Mallorca was better than good. I ate and drank in silence while Pauli launched a barrage of talk at Dehan, and Dehan responded monosyllabically. I looked up when she asked her, "So when you gonna get married, Carmen? A beautiful, smart girl like you should be married! You ain't so young anymore, *chiquilla*!"

Dehan shrugged. "Nobody wants me, Pauli. Who wants a half-Jewish, half-Mexican girl with too much attitude? Huh? Nobody, that's who."

"*Hoy! Chiquilla!*"

"Listen, changing the subject, I wanted to ask you about Rosario."

Pauli looked sad for a moment and sat back in her chair.

"Yeah, you said on the phone, but I don't know what I can tell you, Carmen."

"Detective Stone"—she gestured at me, like Pauli might not know who I was—"heads up a cold-cases team."

I smiled at her with my mouth full of Mallorca and said, "You cam caw me Johng!" She smiled, and I swallowed. "Anyone who makes cake this good can call me John." I winked for good measure, and she blushed prettily. Dehan was giving me her inscrutable look, but I ignored her.

"So, we are reviewing Rosario's case in the light of some new evidence, and I was wondering if you could tell us anything about her friends at that time, who she was hanging out with, if she had a boyfriend . . ."

Pauli became abstracted for a moment, staring out of the window. She shook her head. "I don't like to remember it. Sometimes it seems such a long time ago, and other times it's like yesterday. She went a bit . . ." She waved her hand in circles in the air. "She went a bit crazy around that time." She looked at me and shrugged. "She was smart, and sometimes smart people go crazy, you know? She started hanging around with this communist crowd. I don't know about politics." She waved her hand again, dismissing politics. "But I know that some people who say they are communists . . ." She waggled her head, waggled her hips, and started laughing. "Really, it's not politics what they are doing! They are making parties, taking drugs . . ."

I smiled. "*Cuchi cuchi.*"

She laughed and pointed at me. "That's what they are doing!" She sighed, stopped laughing, and dropped her hands onto her lap. "My poor Rosario, she wanted to live a little. She thought she had met people who were smart like her, you know? But they weren't like her. They were not good people." She gestured at Dehan. "Even your mom, God rest her! You know your mom was open-minded and tolerant, but even she stopped seeing her, because she said to me, 'Pauli, your sister's friends are a bit crazy!' She was worried about her."

I scratched my chin. "What exactly was worrying her, Pauli?" I shrugged and gave her a meaningful look. "Or who?"

She nodded a lot and pointed at me. She said to Dehan, "*El no es tonto! El sabe!*" Which I understood as, "He's not stupid, he knows." Dehan gave a noncommittal shrug, but before she could say anything, Pauli was talking again.

"There was one guy. She was crazy about him. And she told me he was crazy about her too." She started waving her hands around in the air. "Oh! He is wonderful! He is so *handsome*! He is so smart! He is good, and passionate, and committed to his cause, and one day, he is going to be *president*!"

Dehan frowned. "President?"

"That's what she said. You know what I told her? I told her, 'Wake up! Wake up, Rosi! He just wants to get you in bed!' 'No! No! No! We gonna get married! He's in love with me! He's gonna leave his wife! He don't love her anymore!'"

Dehan was nodding. "This guy was married? So, were he and Rosario sleeping together?"

"She told me no! An' I believe her. She always told me everything, and I asked her, 'Rosi! You been sleeping with a married man? Tell me!'" She raised her hands again and made a horrified face, mimicking her sister. "'Nonononooo! Pauli! I never do that! I told him, you want this body?'" She made a coquettish move that made me smile. "'You put a ring on it, boy!'"

She laughed out loud, and we laughed with her. I asked her, "Can you remember his name?"

She puffed out her cheeks and stared at the ceiling, blowing. "It was fourteen, fifteen years ago, but there was only five of them in that group. There was Rosario, Mateo . . ." She nodded. "He was a nice man. I liked him. He was married to that Irish girl, or Scottish . . ." She made a kind of beckoning sign at Dehan with her fingers. "You know her. What was her name? Susanna! They were nice people. I don't know why they hang out with that gang."

I raised an eyebrow. "They were half of that gang. The other half were Mary and . . ."

She cut me short, pointing at me. "Maria and *Eduardo*! I remember now. No, you are right! You are right!" She turned to Dehan again. "I told you, *no es tonto!*" She turned back to me. "Eduardo! He was like the devil. He was a bad influence on people. Everybody follows him and do what he tells them. He was a big success, made lots of money, telling everybody he is a community leader, he is gonna help the Puerto Ricans and the Latinos . . . I think he was selling his soul to the devil!"

"And this was the man she thought was going to marry her?"

"Yes, Eduardo Irizarry."

I scratched my head, and Dehan voiced the question I was about to ask. "So when she was raped and strangled, why didn't the cops investigate Irizarry?"

She made a huge shrug. "Don't ask me! How should I know?"

"Did you tell them about him?"

"Of course! Me and your mom, we told the detective, 'This is the man who done it, for sure! *For sure!* Because she didn't want to go to bed with him!' But nothing happened." She looked embarrassed and put her head on one side. It was a kind of apologetic gesture. "It was different back then. There was a lot of corruption in the cops. People said Eduardo had friends in the precinct." She hesitated. "Look, I show you something."

She got up and went to the sideboard. She opened the cupboard and, crouching down, she pulled out a photo album, which she brought back to her chair. She leafed through it until she came to a particular page. There she stopped and peeled back the cellophane to extract one particular photo. She handed it to Dehan.

"This was one of the last parties they had. It was a barbeque at Eduardo's house. She was excited because there was a police detective there as a guest. She was saying that Eduardo was real well connected. I told her, 'Rosi, that is not a good connection. He is a defense counsel, what's he doing making a barbeque with detectives?' Anyhow, I knew this detective, we all did. He was not a good man . . ."

Dehan stared at me and handed me the picture. They were all about fifteen years younger. There was Sue Mackenzie with a man I guessed was Matt. Mary Irizarry was standing next to a pretty Latino girl whom I assumed was Rosario. Next to her, with his big arm around her, was Ed, holding a beer, and next to him was a big, broad-shouldered hulk of a man in shorts and a floral shirt. Pauli knew him, Dehan knew him, and I knew him. Everybody knew him. It was Mick Harragan, the bent cop who had killed Dehan's parents.

# TWELVE

It was a three-hundred-yard walk to Angela's house, what used to be Rosario's house. It was a walk that Rosario and Pauli must have done a thousand times, and Angela with them—until Rosario had been murdered, murdered for being pretty and fun and attractive and curious.

We walked slowly, Dehan with her hands thrust deep into her pockets, frowning at her feet as she went. "It's not unexpected," she said after a moment. "This was Harragan's beat. He had it sewn up. If Ed was up and coming in the barrio as a defense attorney, he would have sought a connection with Mick Harragan, to keep him sweet. And if Harragan saw a young Puerto Rican making a career for himself as a defense attorney, he would have sought that connection too. For the same reason."

I nodded. "Yeah, they were natural bedfellows. The question is, did Mick rape her, or was it Ed?" I shrugged. "Or somebody completely different. So far we have little more than hearsay."

It was getting warm, and she reached behind her neck and tied her hair into a knot. "Logically," she said, "I doubt Mick did it. He knew the Latino culture pretty well by then, and he knew it was very territorial. He may have been an arrogant son of a bitch, but he was also cunning, and he knew how to manage his patch. Rosario was Ed's. Ed was making a claim in that photograph. Mick was on the outside; so was Ed's wife. Ed was holding Rosario. She was his."

"So Mick would not have intruded on that."

She shook her head. "The fact that he even went along to Ed's barbeque was a gesture of respect. He was acknowledging that Ed carried weight in the 'hood. He wouldn't have messed with his girl."

I nodded again. "Okay, that makes sense."

She shrugged. "I guess he just got sick of waiting."

I glanced at her. "Sick of waiting?"

"Yeah, he kept promising her marriage, he was going to leave his wife, all that BS, and she just kept telling him, 'Sure, when you do that, we'll share a bed.' He got tired of waiting."

"Yes, I guess so."

"After that, Mick Harragan saw to it that the case went cold. He looked out for his pal."

We turned into Bryant Avenue and started in the direction of Angela's house. There was a dark blue BMW parked outside. There was no reason why there shouldn't be, but it caught my eye, and my gut told me there was something wrong. I noticed Dehan had gone quiet. Next thing, she was loping across the road toward the car, and I was running after her. We were maybe a hundred yards away. For a moment, there was the sound of a woman screaming. I was pulling my piece, accelerating. Dehan had her weapon in her hand and had broken into a sprint. Then there was a figure, big, dressed in black, barreling down the steps.

I shouted, "*Stop! Police! Stop!*" He had the passenger door open and he was about to climb in. He stopped and turned to look. I saw he had a ski mask over his face. He thrust out both hands in front of him, leaning on the roof of the car. He had an automatic, and he was taking his time to take aim.

To take aim at Dehan.

She stopped dead, raised her weapon. There was a double crack, almost simultaneous. I powered into Dehan and hurled her to the ground, sprawling on top of her. I didn't stop. I kept sprawling and scrambling to my feet. But I heard the squeal of rubber and the car was away, turning left onto Garrison Avenue.

I turned toward Dehan. "You okay?"

She was getting to her feet, wincing. "Yes."

I ran for the house.

The door was open, and I took the nine steps in two bounds, shouting, *"Police! NYPD! Angela, are you okay?"*

I froze in the hallway, listening. The bright sunshine lay in a twisted oblong at my feet, framing my shadow. I could hear crying. It was coming from upstairs. Another shadow rose up next to mine. Dehan. She came and stood by my side. I gestured at the living room. She covered me and I went in. It was empty. The back room was the same. Dehan checked the kitchen and we made our way up the stairs, weapons drawn and held out in front of us.

The sobbing grew louder. I shouted again, "Angela! This is Detectives Stone and Dehan! Are you alone? Are you hurt?"

We were on a broad landing. There was a restroom on the right, and three bedrooms making a right angle: two in front of us and one on the left. Only one of the doors was open, and that was where the crying was coming from. It was an ugly, guttural noise, like a young child crying convulsively with an adult's voice.

A shadow moved in the doorway, and then Angela stepped out, her mouth twisted with grief, her hair disheveled, her nightgown awry and ripped open, drenched in blood that streamed from a gash in her forehead.

I moved past her and into the room while Dehan holstered her weapon and went to her. The sheet and the pillow were stained with blood. The duvet was twisted and half on the floor. It also had blood on it. I pulled my cell from my pocket and stepped back onto the landing. As I dialed, I said to Dehan, "Get her downstairs, to the living room. Don't touch the blood for now."

Into the phone, I said, "This is Detective Stone. We need a crime scene team at 899 Bryant Avenue; we also need an ambulance."

I followed them downstairs. Angela was leaning on Dehan's shoulder, still sobbing. Dehan settled her on the sofa and knelt in front of her, examining her forehead. I hunkered down beside her to have a look too. There was a two-inch gash above her right eye, and her left cheek was beginning to swell. On closer inspection, I could see she had bruising all over her face and on her upper arms.

Dehan held her hand in both of her own and asked her, "Angela, what happened?"

Angela shook her head, wiping her eyes on the back of her free hand. "I don't know. I was asleep. I took a pill. Then in my dream . . ." She opened her mouth, but no sound came out. She wasn't breathing. When her voice finally came, it was twisted with fear and grief. "I didn't know if it was a dream or what was happening. I couldn't move . . . ! And it hurt so much!"

Dehan got up and sat next to her, with her arm around her shoulders. She glanced at me. "You want to make a cup of tea?"

I nodded and went to the kitchen. While the kettle boiled, I ran over in my mind what I had seen. It wasn't much. The dark blue BMW. I hadn't seen the plate. Then the guy. He came down the nine steps fast, maybe in a single bound. He was big, real big. Not just tall, but powerfully built. I figured at least six three, maybe more. Big shoulders, big arms and legs. Agile. Black jeans, black sweatshirt, black ski mask. I tried to focus more, on his hands, on his eyes, but I couldn't be sure. Dehan had been ahead of me, and by the time I was close enough to make out details, I was concentrating on her, and getting her out of his line of fire.

The kettle clicked, and I poured the boiling water into a mug with a tea bag in it, added two spoons of sugar and a dash of milk. She needed it strong and sweet.

By the time I got back and handed her her tea, she had calmed down a bit. She took it in both hands, and I sat in one of the armchairs.

"It's been a pretty rough couple of days for you, Angela, hasn't it?"

She nodded and shivered, holding the hot mug close. Dehan rubbed her back a couple of times and said, "I'll go and get you a blanket."

She rose and left the room. Angela watched her go. Then she looked back at her mug, avoiding my eyes.

"Do you know who that man was, Angela?"

She shook her head.

"Did you get a look at his face?"

"No, he had the mask on."

"How about the color of his eyes?"

"Black. His eyes, his hands."

"Did he say anything to you?"

Somewhere outside, I heard a siren. It seemed very far away, but I knew it would be here soon. She hesitated, like she was going to tell me something he'd said, but closed her mouth and stared at me for a moment. Then she shook her head.

"No. He didn't say anything."

I sat forward, put my elbows on my knees. "Angela, is this the same man who killed Sebastian?"

Again, the long pause while she looked at me. "I don't know."

"You understand that if it is, you are at risk. You are *seriously* at risk." I shook my head. "I can't protect you unless you help me."

Dehan came in and sat by her side again. She placed a blanket around her shoulder and held her. Outside, the sirens were getting louder. Dehan spoke gently to her.

"What he's saying is true, Angela."

A twist of bitterness contorted Angela's face and she turned to Dehan. "The cops didn't protect my mom, did they? Or yours!"

Dehan didn't flinch. She came right back, "That's why I became a cop." She shifted her ass so that she was facing her and took hold of her left hand in both of hers. "Let me tell you something. A year ago, Detective Stone and I met. He had just formed the cold-cases unit." I raised an eyebrow at the slight inaccuracy, but she ignored me and went right on. "The very first case we worked together, we hunted for the cop who killed my mom, the same cop who allowed your mother's killer to go free." She flicked her eyes at me, and there may have been a smile in there, somewhere. "It didn't work out how we expected, but I learned something about my partner, and about myself. He's a good man that I can trust with my life, and I know that we will both do the right thing, whatever the cost. We *will* protect you, Angela, if you'll let us. If you trust us, we will not let you down. You have my word."

She stared at Dehan for a long moment. Then she looked at me. I tried to look like the kind of man Dehan had described. Outside, the sirens swelled and an ambulance drew up, and just behind it the CSI team. Dehan rose and went out to meet them.

I leaned forward with my elbows on my knees again. "Angela, I want to help you. We'd both like to help you. But the bottom line is, you have no choice. If you don't let us help you, that man is going to keep coming back. We can't let that happen. So if you refuse to help *us*, I will charge you with obstructing justice, and that can carry serious prison time."

She went pale, and I felt bad. But I told myself I'd feel worse if I had to come back to this house and investigate her murder.

She said, "You wouldn't do that . . ."

"You heard what my partner said, Angela. I will do whatever it takes to catch the person who did this to you, and to Luis and Sebastian. I don't want to investigate your murder. I want to put him away before that happens. I want to help you. That's why I am giving you a choice."

She nodded.

Suddenly the room was full of paramedics bustling and pushing, and Joe was at the door with Dehan, calling me. I stood and spoke to the paramedic who was inspecting Angela's wound. "If you're taking her to the hospital, I have to talk to her before she goes." I turned to Joe. "You need to take samples of the blood; it may not all be hers. You also need to print her neck and face. I can't remember if he was wearing gloves. I don't think he was."

One of the CSI guys came in and hunkered down next to the paramedic. I stepped over to Joe. "She was attacked while she was sleeping in the bedroom upstairs. There's quite a bit of blood. Either she has another wound or he has. I don't see it all coming from that gash on her head. Check her fingernails too."

Dehan nodded. "He bolted like he had a jalapeño pepper up his ass. I think he got more than he expected."

I smiled at her. "Graphic."

She grinned. "That's Latinas, Stone, but what would you know?"

She stepped away, back to Angela. I frowned, aware I had been told something but not quite sure what it was. Joe raised an eyebrow at me. "What would you know? I am going to have a look at the crime scene. Catch you later."

I went back to Angela. The chief paramedic was talking to Dehan. He looked at me as I approached. "Detective, I was just explaining to your partner. Angela needs to be seen by a doctor at the hospital. She is in shock, and she may have other injuries that we can't detect here. If you want to take a statement from her, you'll have to do that at the hospital."

I nodded. "Okay. We'll be right behind you."

They took Angela out, and we left the house to Joe and his team. Outside, under the early June sun, I climbed behind the wheel of my old Jaguar while Dehan got in the other side, and we watched the ambulance pull away. For some reason, I kept hearing Dehan's words repeated in my head. "It didn't work out how we expected, but I learned something about my partner, and about myself. He's a good man that I can trust with my life . . ."

For some reason I couldn't explain, those words made me feel a vague sense of loss. I frowned at her and opened my mouth to ask her. But she was on the phone.

"This is Detective Dehan. I need you to trace a license plate and put out an APB . . ."

I closed my mouth again, pulled away after the ambulance, and told myself to get a grip and focus on the job at hand.

On what was important.

# THIRTEEN

She was sitting in bed. A large square of sunlight lay warped across the blanket. She had a large sticking plaster on her forehead, over her right eye, and the bruising on her face and her neck was beginning to come out. She was a pretty girl, but right then she looked a mess. However, she looked calm, and she was able to talk to us.

Dehan sat on the far side of the bed, with the sunlight making a halo around her black hair. I sat on the near side, with my back to the door, watching Angela while she spoke.

"I share the house with my boyfriend, Moses. Moses Johnson. We live together, like we were married. We *are* married, we just don't believe in the church, or the state." She looked at us both in turn, like we might disapprove. "We believe in each other. He's a good man, brave and strong. We want to have kids, raise a family, do what we can to improve the barrio. But it's hard here."

Dehan nodded her agreement. "Where is Moses now?"

Angela bit her lip, stared down at her hands.

"Angela?"

"He's away."

I scratched my chin, then smiled. "That's telling us where he's not. But we need to know where he is. And also, what made him go there."

"He got into some trouble with some people in the neighborhood."

Dehan frowned. "What kind of trouble, Angela?"

"I don't know. He wouldn't tell me. He said it was best if I didn't know."

"You think he might have borrowed money, or got involved in trafficking? Is he moving drugs right now?"

Angela was shaking her head, staring at Dehan. "No! No! Absolutely not! Never! He would never do that! He would rather die than get involved in drugs. He is passionate about that. You don't know him."

I said, "We'd like to. Hunts Point needs people like Moses. Like both of you. Where is he?"

Again the silence, and a big sigh. This was hard for her. "He won't tell me where he is. He said it's for my own good. He's looking for a way so we can both leave."

Dehan nodded like she understood. "But you must be in touch. You must have some way to communicate."

"We call each other, on the phone."

"You have to call him, Angela, and tell him that for your safety, and his, we need to see him. We need to meet with him, very soon."

"I will, I'll call him. I'll let you know what he says."

Dehan sat forward, with her elbows on her knees. "So you think this guy who attacked you was after Moses?"

"I know he was." She looked Dehan in the eye. "He was trying to make me tell him where he was. He said he'd kill me if I didn't."

"Okay, I've asked you this before, but I am going to ask you again, and it is absolutely imperative, Angela, that you tell me the truth. You understand?"

"Yes, of course. I will."

"Do you have any idea who your attacker was?"

She shook her head. "I honestly don't. He was very big, like a giant. He was so heavy, and strong." She paused, breathing slowly to steady her nerves. "He was black, he had an accent. He wasn't Bronx. He sounded maybe . . ." She made a face and shrugged. "Maybe French or Nigerian, something foreign." She stopped again to think. "Like he didn't pronounce his *r*'s. He kept saying, 'Where is Moses?' but instead of 'where' he said it like, 'whe-ah.' Does that help?"

I glanced at Dehan. She glanced at me. I said, "Yeah. It helps a lot. Angela, my next question is really important, more than you maybe realize. What were Sebastian and Luis doing at your house that night?"

Her head tilted on one side. She bit her lip. Tears spilled from her eyes and rolled down her cheek. It was an expression of almost intolerable sadness. She shrugged. "They wanted to party. I didn't want to, but they were happy, joking. They had the next day off. They said they'd been somewhere and they had to leave. That made them laugh. They arrived in a taxi . . ."

I interrupted her. "What time was this?"

"I guess it was maybe thirty minutes after one. I let them in and told them I had no drink. I don't really drink. Neither does Moses. We don't keep drink in the house. They said to let them borrow the car, they'd go to the all-night store. I said no way, but Luis, you know, he always gets his way. He took the keys from the hook in the kitchen. They were laughing and I couldn't make them be serious . . ."

She trailed off. Wiped her eyes with her fingers. I said, "What happened next, Angela?"

"I told them to phone their parents, tell them they were with me and they were going to stay the night. Sleep it off. I would not let them drive while they were drunk. Sebastian agreed. While they called, I made coffee and some eggs. They had some, and after that, Sebastian said he was okay. He wasn't as drunk as Luis. They said they just wanted a few beers and then they'd go to bed. In the end, I agreed."

I thought for a moment. "So at what time did they go out?"

"Maybe two o'clock. Maybe a bit later. They had to go to an ATM to get some money. Then the store . . ."

"So they were gone, what? Forty-five minutes?"

"I guess about that."

"Then what happened?"

"I heard the car pull up outside. I went to the window to see if it was them. It was. But there was another car, over on the right. It had its headlamps on. A guy got out. He was big, tall, he was dressed in black, with a ski mask. He walked up, real quick. Then he had the gun in his hand and he just started shooting through the driver's window. I saw Luis fall out of the passenger side. He staggered a couple of paces, then fell on his knees and tried to crawl up the steps. The guy just walked back to his car and drove away."

Dehan asked her, "Was it the same car as your attacker used today?"

She shook her head. "I didn't see what car he used today."

"Do you think it could have been the same man?"

She thought for a long time before answering. "It's possible. When he attacked me, I was sleeping. Everything is kind of a blur. The night of the shooting, he was outside . . . under the streetlamp, and in the headlamps, he looked big. He was tall. He was dressed in dark clothes. That's all I could make out."

We were quiet for a while. I was trying to fit all the pieces together in my head. The problem was they didn't all fit. I thought of the old cliché about a case fitting together like the pieces of a jigsaw. The problem here was that there seemed to be at least three jigsaws.

I sighed. "We're nearly done, Angela. This is all really helpful. But there is one more thing I need you to clear up for me. The bullet holes in your door. They're not from the same night, they are earlier. What happened there?"

She turned and gazed out the window. After a moment, she wiped a tear from her cheek. Then she reached for a box of tissues on her bedside table, blew her nose, and wiped her eyes again. She gave a small laugh and apologized. "I'm sorry. It's just all so much. I feel kind of overwhelmed."

Dehan smiled. "Take your time. We'll leave you in peace in a minute. I promise."

Angela smiled at her, like she didn't really want her to leave her in peace.

"It was a couple of weeks ago. It was what made Moses decide to move out. We were watching TV. I guess it was about six in the evening. There was a ring at the doorbell and Moses went to open the door. I heard some voices, like Moses was talking to a man. Then all of a sudden there was this shout. It was Moses yelling, 'You get out of my house!' really mad, really angry. I heard a crash, like somebody falling down the stairs. The door slammed. And then, like firecrackers going off. Two of them, and I heard Moses curse in the hallway. When I went out to see what was going on, he was holding his leg and he was bleeding badly."

Dehan spread her hands. It was an eloquent gesture of frustration. "Why didn't you call the cops?"

Angela held her eye for a long moment. "You know why, Carmen."

Dehan looked at me and heaved a big sigh. "Mick."

I nodded. "Angela, I've had a police guard put on your door. When they discharge you, we are going to move you to a safe house until the trial. I want you to call Moses. He can be with you if you want. When we catch whoever did this, I need you both to testify at the trial. Have we got a deal?"

She nodded. "For my part, yes. I'll talk to Moses and convince him to see you and talk to you."

"Good girl." I stood. "Call me as soon as you get an answer. Now get some rest."

We stepped out of the room and I walked toward the elevator, stretching and cracking my vertebrae. Dehan was close behind me, rubbing her eyes. The doors hissed open and we stepped inside. As it began to move down, she shook her head at the floor and said, "What the hell, Stone? What's going on?"

I stared at the ceiling of the elevator. "What's going on? What's going on is that we are going to Emilio's Gourmet Pizza, down the road, for a couple of gourmet pizzas and a couple of beers while we try and untangle this mess."

She stared at her boots like she was disappointed in them. I raised an eyebrow and added, "If you for some reason do not want to join me, and would rather have a beef sandwich at your desk, I'll join you later."

She shook her head. "No. Pizza and beer sounds good."

"You bet your sweet ass it does."

She looked a little startled. I felt a little startled myself, though I didn't show it. The doors opened, and we made our way out to the Jag.

As we pulled onto Morris Park Avenue, headed west, I sighed and gently thumped the wheel with my fist. "The more we find out, the more complicated it gets. It's like two cases. It's like two separate cases, but the separation is in the wrong place."

She frowned. "What do you mean?"

I drummed on the wheel with my fingers as we cruised slowly toward Emilio's. "If we were wrong, and there was no connection between Sebastian's killing and Rosario's, then there should be a degree of coherence in the evidence relating to Sebastian's killing, and then there should be coherence in the evidence relating to Rosario's killing. Right?"

She nodded. "Mm-hm . . ."

"But the *incoherence* all relates to Sebastian and Angela. Who the hell is this guy who attacked her? Why the hell is he after Moses? Did he kill Sebastian because he thought he was Moses? Why'd he do it at three a.m.? Who waits for somebody who leads a quiet life and doesn't drink, *outside* their house, at three a.m.? It doesn't make sense. The chances of their turning up are nonexistent, because at that time of the morning they are going to be inside, in bed!"

"I know."

I pulled up outside Emilio's and we went inside. We sat at a table by the window and I stared out at the Jag while Dehan gave our order. When she was done, I said, absently, still staring at my car but seeing the Toyota with Sebastian's riddled body stretched across the seat, and Luis struggling up the steps toward the door, "All of which means that either the shooter knew they were going to be out in the car, or the shooter planned to go inside, and the killing was opportunistic."

# FOURTEEN

She leaned back in her chair and watched me for a moment till I met her eye.

"Maybe," she said. "Maybe it's simpler than that."

"What do you mean?"

"Maybe we are complicating things unnecessarily. Sometimes you can do that. Not you, necessarily, but one. One can do that. Unnecessarily."

"Complicate things." I smiled.

"Yeah."

"Okay, so how do we uncomplicate them?"

Emilio came over with our beers. When he'd left, Dehan took a pull, settled the glass carefully on the table, and licked the foam from her top lip.

"Sebastian and Luis finish work and go back to Lynda Graham's house. They start partying, they get drunk, yadda yadda. At some point Jack turns up. Maybe he spoils the vibe, maybe he doesn't, whatever, come one o'clock the boys leave. They still feel like partying, so they decide to go to Angela's place. Maybe they know she's alone. Either way, they get a taxi and get there in the small hours. Nobody is stealing from the hospital, nobody is encroaching on anybody's turf. Just two nice med students letting off steam with an old friend."

I nodded. "Okay, so far I like it."

She nodded back at me. "I like Angela as a mother hen to her almost-brothers. I can believe that. It sounds right and it fits with what I know of her, her mom, and—hey!—her culture. That's what a lot of nice Latina girls are like: mother hen."

"I believe you, stay on task."

"I am. So she fusses over them, gives them coffee, etcetera. Just like she told it. Cut. Meanwhile, down at the ranch, two weeks earlier, Moses, somehow, in some way we do not yet know, has upset Mr. X." She leaned forward, spread her hands like she was doing a magic trick. "We don't know yet who Mr. X is."

"That's why you called him Mr. X."

"Right. But he is big, he is bad, and he is dangerous to know. Moses knows him and somehow he has fallen foul of him. He turns up two weeks ago to settle whatever score it is they have. Moses throws him down the stairs. He shoots through the door, hits Moses in the leg. Moses leaves town. Mr. X doesn't know that. And what happens that night is pure, simple, bad luck. The boys turn up. She makes them coffee. They persuade her to let them use the car. Meanwhile, Mr. X turns up outside. He arrives maybe seconds before they come back from the store. He is *planning* to break in and kill Moses, but to his surprise he sees the Toyota arrive and park. As you demonstrated yourself that morning, the visibility was shit. He can't see through the windshield, but he has no reason to believe that there is anybody else but Moses and Angela in the car. He has no beef with Angela. So he gets out of his vehicle, he walks over, empties his magazine through the window. Exactly as you said, he does not go and finish Angela because he does not care about her. As far as he is concerned, he has killed Moses. He goes back to his car and leaves."

"So, how . . ."

She raised a hand. "Wait! I'm on a roll. He hears through the

Bronx grapevine that the two people shot that morning on Bryant Avenue were two medical students, and not Moses and Angela. Maybe he hears also that Moses has vamoosed."

"Vamoosed."

"Yeah. So he goes back, mad, crazy, and assaults her, asking her where Moses is. She screams the house down. He runs. We arrive. QED. I rest my case."

I took a deep breath, pulled off half my beer, and set the glass down carefully on the ring it had left on the table. Dehan flopped back in her chair and spread her hands.

"Come on, Stone, it covers *everything*!"

The pizzas arrived. Emilio wished us *buon appetito* and left us to it. I folded a slice of pizza, bit it, and chewed, thinking carefully. After a bit, I nodded.

"You're right. It covers everything; it is simple and it is elegant."

She narrowed her eyes at me. "You just know, you just *know* there is a 'but' coming."

I smiled. "It is your own but, so to speak."

"The sweet one you mentioned in the elevator?"

I smiled. "The very same." I stuffed the crust in my mouth and spoke. "Whamph abou Wosawio?" I swallowed and drank beer while she watched me, then repeated, "What about Rosario?"

She looked out the window and shook her head. "Mother . . ."

I spread my hands. "There is something missing, Dehan. I think you're right. I think you are right in practically everything you said. But there is one small detail, one small thing where it is different. I don't know what it is. Not yet. But . . ." I paused, stared out at the Jag, watched the traffic pass, the people on the sidewalk, tried to think what that "but" led to.

"What? But what?"

I looked her in the eye. "Whoever killed Sebastian, also killed Rosario. And Mr. X did not kill Rosario."

She stared at me a long time. "I am ninety-nine percent certain that Ed Irizarry killed Rosario."

I thought about it, then shrugged and folded another piece of pizza. "Then, if you're right, Ed Irizarry killed Sebastian."

"The boy he thought was leading his own son astray."

I bit, chewed, shrugged, and nodded.

She went on, "The son of the woman he raped and murdered. The connection is there."

I smiled. "Yeah, the connection is there. All that's missing are the facts and the evidence. And, while we're at it, a motive."

We ate in silence for a while, thinking. Then Dehan's phone rang. She pulled it from her pocket, stuck it to her ear, and said, "Yumph?" She listened for a bit, then swallowed and said, "Wait!" She laid out a paper napkin and made hand gestures at me to give her my pen. I did, and she made a note on the napkin. Then she said, "How do you spell that? A-K-A-C-H-U-K-W-U, Akachukwu. Okay. Put out an APB on him, will you? Thanks." She hung up, looked at me. "The bimmer, registered to one Akachukwu Oni, a Nigerian national living in New York with a rap sheet as long as . . ."

"An elephant's trunk?"

"That is probably racist."

"Probably. What kind of rap sheet?"

"Trafficking mainly, drugs, guns, prostitution, but also assault and assault with a deadly weapon. Many of the charges are from Nigeria, where it seems he was let off for no discernible reason. Here he's been charged several times but always got off when witnesses failed to show, or changed their testimony before the trial."

I nodded. "Good. We are getting somewhere. Let's go talk to this Akachukwu."

Dehan stuffed a piece of pizza in her mouth and said, "Apparently it means 'Hand of God.'"

I drained my beer. "Do you know what Carmen means?"

She made a face and shook her head.

"It means 'Vineyard of the Gods.' It might also mean 'poem,' and is the origin of the English word 'charm.'"

She raised her eyebrows, said, "Huh," then frowned at me. "You know this why?"

I stood. "I looked it up. You got an address for the Hand of God?"

"Yeah. It's an apartment over the Lotus Garden, a Chinese restaurant on the corner of Randall Avenue and Bryant. Two gets you twenty he isn't there and never has been."

"You're probably right, but it's a place to start. Let's go."

We stepped out into the street. I stopped, with my car keys in my hand, and looked up at the vast, blue sky. "There is," I said, "no apparent connection between Akachukwu and Ed Irizarry." I looked at Dehan, who was leaning against my car, waiting. "And there should be, Little Grasshopper. There should be."

We went to his apartment. The street door to the stairs was locked up, and the windows showed no signs of life. We asked in the Chinese restaurant under the apartment and the owner told us nobody lived up there, she used it as a storeroom. I had been wrong. It wasn't a place to start. It was a dead end, and all we could do was wait: wait for a patrol car to spot either the BMW or Akachukwu, wait for the lab to work through the forensic evidence, wait and hope that Luis would regain consciousness.

Not for the first time, Dehan spoke my thoughts as we climbed back into the Jag.

"Let's get back to the station house, Stone. I want to review Rosario's case file and see if I can find any link with this case."

"There is something we are not seeing, Dehan. It's there, right in front of our noses, but we are not seeing it."

———

BACK AT THE STATION, we didn't get very far with Rosario's case file. We had just pulled it and started reading when the desk sergeant buzzed me.

"Yeah, Maria, what's up?"

"You ain't going to believe it, Detective, but Akachukwu Oni is here. He says he thinks you might be looking for him."

"Okay, don't let him leave." I hung up and stood. "Akachukwu. He's here."

Dehan's eyebrows rose up to her hairline. "*What?*"

"Let's go get him!"

We pushed out to the front desk. The sergeant indicated Akachukwu with her head, but she needn't have bothered. He was unmistakable. He was leaning against the wall, watching us with dead eyes. He was six six if he was an inch, and built like a barn. But there was no fat on him. It was all solid muscle. I am not easily scared, but this man was terrifying. I tried not to let him see I thought so, stepped over, and said, "Are you Akachukwu Oni?"

He didn't move, just watched me with his expressionless eyes. His voice was exceptionally deep. He said, "Yes."

Dehan covered him and I turned him to face the wall.

"Akachukwu Oni, I am placing you under arrest for aggravated assault on Angela Rojas and the attempted murder of Detective Carmen Dehan. You don't have to say anything, but whatever you do say will be taken down in evidence and used against you in a court of law."

He placed his hands behind his back, and as I cuffed him, he said, "I am here to cooperate."

We frisked him. He was unarmed, and we took him up the stairs to interview room one. There we sat him down on a chair and manacled him to the table. He dwarfed everything around him, made the furniture look like nursery toys. We sat opposite, and I studied his face for a moment, trying to fit this new piece into an already incomprehensible puzzle.

I said, "You are entitled to have an attorney present . . ."

"I know my rights, Detective. I am not ignorant. I have already told you I want to cooperate. I do not need a lawyer."

"Okay. What do you want to find Moses Johnson for?"

He blinked. It was the slow blink of a giant iguana. "I am not looking for Moses Johnson."

I frowned. "That's not what Angela Rojas says. She says that when you beat her up, you asked where Moses was. What do you want with Moses, Akachukwu?"

"She is mistaken. I did not attack her, and I did not ask her about Moses."

Dehan leaned her elbows on the table. She was frowning. She looked like she was having trouble believing what was happening. I knew how she felt. It was hard to escape the feeling we were being played somehow.

"Are you denying that you were at Angela's house? Because we saw you, and you shot at us."

He stared at her a long moment before answering. He managed to make expressionless look insolent as his eyes traveled over her face and her body.

"No. I was there. I went to visit and see if she was okay. Neighbors must look out for each other. She did not open the door, so I left."

"You shot at us, Akachukwu!"

He gave a small shrug. "I have enemies. You came running at me, with your guns. I shot in self-defense. I did not know you were police. If I had known you were police, I would have stopped." He spread his hands. "You see, I am here. When I heard you were looking for me, I came of my own free will. I have nothing to hide."

"Why were you wearing a ski mask?"

"I was not." He smiled. It was not a nice thing to see. "You mistake my black face for a ski mask."

I gave a small laugh and smiled on the wrong side of my face, where it looks sarcastic instead of ironic. "Akachukwu, you left traces of DNA at the scene. It's being analyzed as we speak. It would go a lot easier for you if you confess."

He gave me that direct, lifeless stare, and I knew I was looking at a killer, a man who had no empathy and no compassion at all.

"I cannot confess," he said. "I have nothing to confess. You will not find my DNA at the scene of your crime, because I was not there."

I was momentarily disarmed. I didn't know how to tackle this guy. He was as cool as four rocks in a dry martini. With an olive. I shook my head at him and narrowed my eyes.

"You cannot be serious. There is no way you can walk away from this. You are going down for the attempted murder of a cop, Akachukwu. You need to cooperate."

"You are mistaken, Detective. There will be no trial, because you have no evidence. You have no case against me. I will walk free."

# FIFTEEN

I WAS SURPRISED TO SEE DEHAN smiling.

"Okay, we'll see how that plays out. Let's talk about something else."

He regarded her with the same dead expression he'd given me, and spoke in his slow, deep, deliberate voice. "What do you want to talk about? I want to cooperate."

"Why did you kill Sebastian Acosta?"

"I don't know who Sebastian Acosta is. I don't know if I killed him or not. If I did, I do not know why, because I do not know who he is."

Dehan now combined her smile with a frown. "You sweet on Angela? Is that it? You like Angela and you want her for yourself? That's why you've been giving Moses a hard time? Maybe . . ." She leaned back in her chair and crossed her arms. "Maybe you thought that Sebastian was getting it on with Angela while Moses was away."

"I don't know who Sebastian Acosta is."

"He's the guy you shot five times in Angela's car the night before last. Shortly before three in the morning, you walked up to the car outside her house and you shot him through the window, twice in the head, three times in the chest."

He took a moment to study her face. His expression would have been one of curiosity if he hadn't looked so detached. Eventually, he said, "At three o'clock in the morning, the night before last, I was in bed, at my house."

I said, "In the apartment over the Lotus Garden, on Randall Avenue and Bryant?"

"I don't live there. I have a house on Crotona Park. That is where I live."

"Why is your car registered there?"

"I have not got around to changing it."

Dehan raised an eyebrow at him. "Is there anyone who can confirm you were at home in bed at that time?"

His eyes were hooded, half-closed. His smile was one of the most unpleasant things I had ever seen, and he held it on her for a long time. "Of course," he said. "Three of my girlfriends can confirm that they were with me."

"What are their names?"

His eyes glazed, like she'd made an unreasonable request. "I cannot remember every name . . . July, Zoe . . ." He did what should have been a leer but lacked the necessary humanity. "Maybe Carmen?" He shrugged. "They are at my house now. You can go there and get them to make a statement."

I looked at her and nodded. "Send a car over. Get them to take detailed statements, twelve hours between seven p.m. and seven a.m."

She nodded and left the room. The door closed, and we were left in silence. He watched me with a complete absence of any kind of emotion or expression. I decided on a different tack.

"You have any family in New York, Akachukwu?"

"I have no family. They are all dead."

"Friends . . . ?"

"I am not a refugee, Detective. I am not looking for a green card. I am a businessman. I live here because it is good for my business. I bring a lot of money into the U.S., and I pay my taxes."

"What kind of business?"

He leaned forward, focused hard on my face, and there was death and pleasure in his eyes. "I buy and I sell, Detective Stone. That is what all business is. Buy and sell."

"What do you buy and sell?"

"Whatever will give me a profit." He sat back, and now his smile became a huge grin. "If it is legal."

"You have a long record of arrests, Akachukwu."

"But no convictions. A businessman like me, in Africa, has many opportunities to make a lot of money. But he must tread a very fine line between what is legal and what is not legal. Tell me something, Detective Stone. Why do you call me Akachukwu?"

I frowned. "Because that's your name."

His face went dead again, but there was an indefinable danger in his expression, and I found myself glancing at his cuffs to make sure they were still on. "My name," he said, "to you, is Mr. Oni. I do not call you John and Carmen, so why do you call me Akachukwu? For the same reason you assume I am a refugee, an immigrant looking for one of your green cards. But I am a very rich, successful man, Detective Stone, and I pay my taxes like I told you, so you should show me some respect and call me Mr. Oni."

"Do you trade in drugs and weapons, Mr. Oni?"

"Only if it is legal."

"Were you ever in the army . . . Mr. Oni?"

"I was in the Nigerian army, and after that I was a mercenary for six years. I made a lot of money, killing people legally, Detective. And then I started my business, buying and selling all kinds of marketable goods, all over the world, as long as they were legal."

"Do you sell services as well?"

He shook his head slowly. "No. No services."

"Mr. Oni, somebody fitting your description was seen by a witness approaching Angela's car the night before last, at shortly before three, and opening fire into that car, killing Sebastian Acosta."

"A lot of black men are big, tall, and strongly built. Tell me something, Detective, this man who was seen, was he wearing a ski mask?" I didn't answer. He smiled again. "If he was, that would make him very hard to identify, and you saying he fit my description just makes you sound racist."

"How did you know he was wearing a ski mask?"

He shrugged. "I didn't. But I have seen my fair share of violence in life, Detective. The killing you described sounds like a professional hit to me, and most people doing a professional hit in a populated area, even late at night, will wear a ski mask. Wouldn't you agree? So, it was a fair guess."

I had a couple of uniforms take him down to the cells and went to look for Dehan. I found her halfway up the stairs, leaning against the wall and talking on the phone. She gestured me to keep going and fell into step beside me. ". . . and this was the night before last? At what time . . . ?" She glanced at me. "Around two a.m. Thank you, ma'am. If you don't mind, we'll send somebody over to take a statement . . . Thank you."

We'd arrived at our desks. She sat, screwed up her face, and rubbed it furiously with her hands. I waited till she'd opened her eyes again and said, "What?"

"That was Lynda Graham's next-door neighbor."

I made a face of curiosity and surprise and dropped into my chair. "Really?"

"Night before last, she complained to Lynda about the party going on till the early hours. Lynda told her to take a hike. She says she called the cops and a car came around. By that time the boys had gone, but she said there was another man who turned up, there was a violent row, she's pretty sure the guy was beating up on Lynda, though she can't be certain. When the cops arrived, Lynda told them there was no problem and they would keep it down. Shortly after that, the guy left in a dark sedan."

"And around and around we go . . . I seem to remember once before we had too many suspects. And that time the answer was staring us in the face too. Okay, we'll leave Akachukwu, Mr. Oni, to meditate on his future for a while, and go and have another talk with Lynda and maybe Jack."

I went to stand but she was giving me a funny look. "You mind taking this one on your own, Stone?"

I frowned at her. "Why?"

"You said before that you wanted to review Rosario's case file. You keep saying we're missing something that is staring us in the face. I think you're right, and I think it has to do with Rosario. If you don't need me, then I'd like to review her case, in detail. Maybe the thing we are missing is in that file."

I stared at her for a long moment, then said, "I need you."

She looked momentarily startled.

I smiled. "But I agree you should review her case. Call me if you find anything."

She watched me stand and leave, without answering.

In the car, on the way to Lynda's house, I kept going over in my mind how she had seemed when we spoke to her. She hadn't looked like a woman who had been beaten up in the last few hours. The absence of bruising didn't say much. Men who are in the habit of hitting women soon learn to strike where it doesn't show. But it was a different kind of bruising that was missing with Lynda: a bruising of the mind and soul, a latent fear that you can see in the eyes, that tells you she has grown accustomed to wincing and cowering. It was a bruising I had seen in Mary Irizarry, but not in Lynda Graham.

When I got there and rang on the bell, she opened the door almost immediately. She looked surprised to see me. She also looked up and down the road to see where Dehan was.

I smiled. "I'm on my own, may I come in?"

"Course! You want a grog? Or are you on duty?"

"I'm on duty. I don't want anything, thank you. Can we sit down, please, Lynda?"

She gave a little frown. "Sure. Go ahead." She gestured at a chair and we both sat.

"Lynda, if I take you down to the station, and have a female police officer, or a doctor, examine your body, will they find bruises?"

She sighed and made a face like I was being a pain in the ass. "No. Has Mrs. Paglieri been on at you? Look, the party went on a little too long, things got a little wild . . ."

"I thought you didn't remember . . ."

She closed her eyes. "All right, you caught me. I'm sorry. My delightful neighbor complained. Two very polite coppers came around, asked us to keep it down. By that time, the boys had already left."

"And?"

"And that's it."

I felt a wave of irritation and fought to control it. "Come on, Lynda! Do I look stupid? What car does Jack drive?"

She closed her eyes again and sighed. "This is so fucked up. He drives a clapped-out old BMW . . ."

"What color?"

"Black. He phoned me. It was late, I don't know, around one I guess. It was at the same time as that bitch next door complained. He wanted to know if the guys had left. He could hear the music and Luis and Sebastian laughing. He got mad and said he was coming 'round. I told him not to. Then the bionic bitch said she'd called the police. So that was all kind of a downer? And Seb and Luis left. Two minutes later Jack turns up, like a fucking raving lunatic, and starts shouting at the door. I knew the cops were coming, so I dragged him inside. He was still shouting his fucking head off when they arrived. I mean, where does he fucking get off? He's not even my boyfriend."

"So what happened?"

"They told us to keep it down. I told them we would. They left, and after a while Jack left."

"How much of a while?"

She shrugged and sagged. "I'm just shit with time, you know? I guess it might have been about two? Half two?"

"Two or two thirty. He didn't hit you?"

"He wouldn't fucking dare!"

"You should have told us this when we first spoke to you, Lynda. It is not smart lying to the cops. Have you seen Jack since?"

She shook her head. "No. I think he's kind of ashamed?"

I stood. "How old are you, Lynda?"

She looked surprised at the question. "Twenty-seven, why?"

I reached for the door. "Because it's about time you started growing up?"

Her cheeks went pink, and I stepped out into the sunshine, feeling unreasonably mad.

It was a short walk to Jack's house. All the way, I tried to imagine him holding a gun and shooting Sebastian through the window of the Toyota that night. Sexual passion of one sort or another is the prime motivation for murder—it always has been and always will be. Sex and murder go together like oysters and champagne. And in some ways Jack fit the bill better than Akachukwu—at least for my money. But, I thought sourly as I turned into his street, the fact was that nobody really fit the bill in this case. It was all wrong. The whole damn thing was wrong.

There was a beaten-up old black BMW parked outside his house. I rang the bell and for good measure rang two more times. There was no reply. I peered through the window, but it was hard to see anything clearly. It was when I went back to ring again that I noticed that the wrought iron outer door was not locked. I opened it using my pen and hammered on the inner door with my knuckles. I had a look around. There was no one to see me, so I took out my Swiss Army knife, selected the screwdriver, and, with a firm thump, inserted it into the lock and turned. The lock gave, and I opened the door. I stood a moment in the small hallway. It was very still and very quiet.

"Mr. O'Brien?" There was no reply, so I called louder, "*Mr. O'Brien?*"

There was still no reply, not a sound in the whole house. The door to the living room was on the left. It was ajar, and I eased it open all the way with my foot. My stomach lurched and I turned away, struggling not to vomit. The stench was overpowering, but worse than the smell was what was lying on the carpet in the middle of the floor. I went outside and steadied myself, taking deep breaths. After a moment, I pulled out my cell and called Dehan.

"Yeah."

"I need you here, at Jack O'Brien's house. We need a crime scene team, the ME, and a meat wagon."

"O'Brien's dead?"

"If he's not, he's got real problems. He's been disemboweled. It's the ugliest thing I ever saw, Dehan. It's bad, real bad."

"Okay, I'm on my way."

# SIXTEEN

I STEPPED INSIDE AGAIN AND FORCED MYSELF TO LOOK at the grotesque mess on the floor. His body was bent back at an impossible angle, achievable only because all of his abdominal muscles had been severed. Everything that should have been on the inside was lying on the carpet: a ghastly gray-pink mess, covered in dry, black, clotted blood, and crawling with bluebottles. I tried to ignore the surreal madness of what I was seeing. Tried to read the crime scene instead. What had happened here? What had been the sequence of events?

The iron gate was unlocked. It had not been relocked. That suggested something that had happened at speed. Somebody had rung at the door. He had come and opened it, and whoever it was had entered quickly, forcefully, without bothering to close the gate. Jack would have backed into the house. His attacker would have followed him. What next?

The front door would have swung closed. They are in the entrance hall. Jack is backing away, into the living room. His attacker follows. Jack is big, and tough, a rugby player. For him to be backing away, that means his assailant is either bigger, or armed. Hard to be much bigger, so I go with armed. If he has a gun, he now swaps for a blade. A very sharp blade.

I stopped, analyzing the scene, ignoring the nausea I was feeling, scanning the room. The chairs and lamps were not overturned. The TV was not disturbed. Nothing—*nothing*—was disturbed. The attack was swift, brutal, and utterly deadly. There was no fight. This big, tough, British rugby player just stood there and got killed.

So if the attacker had a gun, he put it away, pulled a blade—what blade? Considering the distance, considering Jack's size and strength, considering that he didn't even get to try and defend himself, it's either a samurai sword or . . .

Or a machete.

A machete, up the sleeve of a jacket or a coat, dropped into the hand, one step, one swipe, and Jack was disemboweled. And then beaten brutally—and unnecessarily, because he was already dead—to end up in that horrific position, broken, practically bisected.

His voice came back to me. One of the last things he'd said to us when we'd come to see him: ". . . Never mind what you'd do to me . . . it's what the hard nuts 'round here would do to me. I been warned . . ."

*The hard nuts 'round here.*

I looked at the door that led down to the cellar. It was open. I went and hunkered down and, as I looked closer, I saw traces of dirt on the carpet. Using my pen, I eased the door open. The light was on, and the smell of cannabis was strong and unmistakable. But I knew we wouldn't find any down there. Whoever had cut Jack down had also taken his plants. I wondered how many he'd had. Twelve? Fifteen? Twenty? Anything between twenty and fifty grand's worth on the street. And he thought the hard nuts would not object to that. He didn't realize, they weren't hard. They were just greedy, and placed no value on human life. They'd have killed him for a hundred bucks, let alone fifty grand.

The distant wail of sirens reached me. I peered at the bare wooden steps. There was dirt that had been spilled from the plants, but there was also a layer of dust, and in it the prints left behind by heavy boots. At a guess, a size twelve or thirteen. A tall man. A big man.

I stood and stepped away from the cellar door, staring hard at the dirty old carpet, visualizing the track to the door, and a guy carrying marijuana plants back and forth. Outside, cop cars started arriving. Through the living room window, I saw the urgent pulse of the red-and-blue lights. I went to open the door.

Dehan was there, walking toward me. Uniforms were spilling from the vehicles, a sergeant was telling them to seal the area around the house, the gurney was being unloaded from the wagon. Frank was suiting up; so were Joe and his team. Dehan said, "What?"

I shook my head. "Brace yourself. It's ugly. He's been practically cut in half."

She suppressed a wince. "He didn't deserve that."

"No. Don't go in just yet, I want to talk to Joe." Joe was moving toward us with his guys. I beckoned him to follow me through the front door and called to the sergeant too. Dehan was close behind, listening. I talked as I went, pointing at the floor. "I think the killer took a number of marijuana plants from the basement out to a vehicle. At a guess, he must have done the trip at least six times, probably more. He's spilled dirt on the stairs and then trodden in it. So he has left boot prints all the way along. I need to know his shoe size, the make of his boots, and if he was alone or there was somebody helping him. Sergeant, start knocking on doors. Somebody saw him loading up a vehicle with cannabis plants."

"I'm on it, Detective."

The team went to work on the basement steps and the carpet. Frank came in as we moved out of the doorway. He stood in the entrance to the living room, staring down at the horrible, inhuman mess on the floor.

"I can honestly say I have never seen anything quite like this. In all my years . . ."

Dehan looked and turned away. Her skin had turned a pasty gray color. I said, "You need to step outside?"

She shook her head.

"Come, I want to have a look upstairs."

We climbed the steps to the upper floor. There was a small landing, a john, and two bedrooms. The back bedroom was jumbled with everything from boxes to bicycle parts. It seemed to be an improvised storeroom, which didn't yield much in the way of information. The front bedroom was also chaotic but was clearly where he slept. The bed was rumpled and unmade. The sheets looked overdue for a wash. There was a TV on a bookcase at the foot of the bed, several dirty plates on the bedside table by the door, a couple of empty beer bottles, and a couple of dirty glasses. All—plates, bottles, and glasses—contained butt ends of what looked like joints. We moved into the room and Dehan stood looking around. "Where the hell do you begin? What a slob!"

On the far bedside table I saw what I had not seen downstairs. A telephone. It was a hunch—not even that, a vague feeling: I saw them, him and Lynda, shouting at each other, both drunk, both mad, both caught up in their toxic, dependent, overemotional relationship. I stood staring at the phone but seeing the scene play itself out, and spoke aloud.

"He didn't hit her. To be honest, Dehan, my gut tells me she'd be more likely to hit him. When he left her house the night before last, he did one of two things. Either he went to Angela's house and killed Sebastian . . ."

She interrupted me. "Which would mean he had a gun, and knew they were going there . . ."

I nodded. "Or, he came home. They are both drunk, both hooked on each other, both making each other unhappy, but needing each other . . ."

I sat on the bed and pressed the messages button. There were six new, and three saved. The new ones were all people asking for dope. He must have been doing a good trade. The first of the saved messages was from Friday night, more precisely, two fifty on Saturday morning. It was Lynda, crying, speaking with that wet, swollen voice of alcohol-induced tears.

"Jack baby, are you there . . . ? Please pick up, lover boy . . . don't be mean. Look, I'm sorry . . . just . . ."

The message was cut short. I looked at Dehan. We had both heard it. Just before it was cut short, Jack's voice, with that same wet, sobbing sound, saying, "Lynda, I'm here, darlin' . . ."

Dehan sighed. It was a big, depressed sigh, and she followed it up with a heartfelt, "Fuck . . ."

"He was here talking to Lynda while Sebastian and Luis were getting shot."

She shook her head. "I never really believed . . . What a waste, Stone."

I nodded. "A stupid waste. He was a nice guy." We stared at each other for a long time. Neither of us said anything, but we were both thinking it, and we both knew we were thinking it.

She turned and made for the bedroom door. I stood and followed. At the bottom of the stairs, I paused to look one more time at what was left of Jack O'Brien. They were preparing to load him onto the gurney, and that was something I couldn't watch. Dehan was standing in the open doorway, breathing deeply. I was about to join her when Joe came up beside me.

"John, I can't be sure till we get this all back to the lab, but we may have something here." He hesitated. "Is this related to Sebastian and Luis' case?"

I nodded. "I think so."

"I know Frank was kind of mentoring Sebastian, so we're giving this . . ." He shrugged. "An unofficial priority."

"I appreciate that, and I know he will too. What have you got?"

"By the looks of it, he had over a dozen plants down there, and there are two sets of footprints, his and somebody who appears to have removed the plants."

"Good."

"Whoever that was seems to have been a very large man, and there is something distinctive about his boot print. I am pretty sure I can trace the manufacturer, but more important than that, John, is that because of the way he walks, he has worn down the heel in a distinctive way. In addition to that, at some point he has trodden on a nail or a piece of glass, or something sharp, and it has etched a unique mark into his heel. This kind of wear and tear can make a shoeprint as unique as a fingerprint."

Dehan had approached us from the door. She frowned. "You can tell all that from the prints in the dust?"

He smiled. "No, but you should have a look down there. A lot of dirt was spilled around the area where he had the plants under the lamps. He left some very clear prints, and we can work them up at the lab. I'll send you the pictures ASAP." As an afterthought, he added, "The guy you have in custody, send me his boots and I'll run a comparison on my own time."

"I'll have them sent over to you now. Thanks, Joe. I appreciate that."

I went outside, sat on the hood of one of the patrol cars, and made the call. When I was done, I crossed my arms and stared at Dehan. She had her hands in her front pockets, and she was chewing her lip and kept standing on tiptoes.

I said, "He told us he'd been warned. You remember that?"

She nodded.

I jerked my head at the house. "Somebody is trying to make a reputation for himself. I've never seen that before, disemboweling somebody like that for growing weed. That's new."

"I agree. It also makes clear that our initial theory is a total washout, which narrows our suspects down to Akachukwu and Ed Irizarry." She sighed and gave her head a little sideways twist, like I'd asked her a question and she didn't know how to answer. "We have a lot of reasons to be thinking about Akachukwu right now, and his alibi, as far as I am concerned, isn't worth a drunken promise . . ."

"A drunken promise, Dehan? That's very poetic."

She ignored me. "But then again, as for Ed, that has one big plus for me."

"It ties in to Rosario's murder. Somehow. We don't know how."

She was nodding as I spoke. "Plus, Stone, the only motive Akachukwu has for killing the boys is if he's sweet on Angela, and frankly we have zero evidence to support that notion. All we know is that he was looking for Moses because he has some kind of grudge. But there is zilch connecting him to Sebastian or Luis."

I thought about that for a while, then shrugged. "I agree with you, but the case against Ed Irizarry, if it can be dignified with that name, is almost as weak. We have no motive for him at all. All we have is a series of bizarre coincidences."

She made a face. "But he has made it clear that he had some kind of grudge against Sebastian."

I had to admit that was true. "Did you manage to look into Rosario's case, by the way?"

"Yeah." She started to pace slowly up and down the sidewalk, three steps one way, then three the other and back again, examining each step as she went. "Forensic evidence was collected, obviously by the CSI team. She was raped and they found semen. A DNA profile of the rapist was produced, but they got no matches on the database. Also, she was bludgeoned with a heavy, blunt object and then strangled. So they used RTX to get prints from her neck and throat. But the prints were poor quality."

She stopped pacing and turned to face me.

"Aside from running the DNA profile, Harragan made no attempt to match the sample with anybody else. He didn't take any swabs from anybody, and claimed he had no suspects. He said it was a random home invasion."

"Okay, that's good. I think with Sue's testimony and Pauli's corroboration we have enough to get a DNA sample from Ed. We'll ask nicely, but if he says no, we can get a warrant. That will at least tie him to Rosario's murder. But what we are still lacking is a concrete connection with Sebastian." I shook my head. "It just isn't enough that he feels he is holding Luis back." I spread my hands. "We *know*, from Frank, that Luis was doing well. His career was not in jeopardy, Sebastian was not a risk to Luis. Ed had no reason to kill him. At least, no reason that we are aware of as yet."

She gave it some thought, then made a face. "Okay, so let's pull him in, scare the bejaysus out of him with the DNA sample, and see if he'll tell us what that connection with Sebastian is."

"Yeah, let's do that. But Dehan, we are still missing something: something key and something obvious."

She smiled. "Come on, Sensei, let's go scare Ed."

I stood and we started to walk back toward my car in the next street. "What's the word on Akachukwu's alibi, by the way?"

She rolled her eyes. "He has about five women living there. They all confirm he was at home that night, and three of them say they shared his bed."

I snorted. "What a dawg."

"Yeah, that's what I call a real man. Not afraid to commit."

I raised an eyebrow she did not see because she was looking away. "Why, Dehan, is that bitterness I hear?"

"Me? What have I got to be bitter about?"

# SEVENTEEN

EDUARDO IRIZARRY WAS NOT A HAPPY MAN. He threatened us with everything from phone calls to the mayor, who, he implied, was a good friend of his golfing buddy's brother's cousin, to lawsuits against the city and us, individually; as well as appeals to friends who were, he suggested, in a position to make our lives very uncomfortable. And he really did mean uncomfortable. He assured us of that.

We sat opposite him in interview room three and waited for his tirade to subside.

"I am an influential man, not without connections in this city!"

I tried to look chastened and asked, "What is it, exactly, Mr. Irizarry, that you object to in our conduct of this case?"

"You are harassing and persecuting us, implying that my son was involved in theft and drugs, insinuating God knows what . . . !"

I sighed heavily. "I apologize, without reservation." He looked suspicious, but I spread my hands and said, "Sometimes our job is very difficult, and we are required to do things that can be very upsetting for the families of victims. However, that is no excuse for having upset you and your wife at this extremely difficult time.

On my own behalf, my partner's, and the department's, Mr. Irizarry, I am very sorry if we have upset or inconvenienced you."

He stared at me, grunted, and asked, "Well, what do you want?"

I sighed. "This is turning out to be a very complicated case, sir —very complicated indeed—and we would be genuinely grateful for some guidance." I stopped and gestured at him with my open hand. "Would you care for some coffee?" I smiled. "I know you appreciate a good coffee, Mr. Irizarry. I do myself. I can get you a cup of freshly ground Colombian instead of the stuff from the machine . . ."

He shrugged and straightened his jacket. "Well, if you have some decent coffee . . ."

I looked at Dehan. "Would you mind, Carmen? The good stuff . . ."

She smiled at Ed, said, "Sure," and got up and left. When she'd left, I leaned back in my chair and frowned.

"How well did you know Mick Harragan?"

The question caught him off guard, and he studied my face a long time before deciding how to answer.

"I knew him."

"Oh, I know that, Mr. Irizarry. I was just wondering how well you knew him. Was he a part of your social circle, for example?"

He gave an astonished laugh. "Hardly! I was building myself a career as a champion of the oppressed Puerto Rican and Latino section of the community in the Bronx. It would hardly have been wise to befriend an Irish cop like Mick Harragan!"

I nodded vigorously, like I agreed with him one hundred percent. "Exactly!" I said. "That is precisely what I thought you would say, and it makes perfect sense. Detective Dehan and I were the team who exposed Mick Harragan's corruption."

The door opened, and Dehan came in with a china mug of aromatic coffee. She smiled as she set it down in front of him. "Forgive the inelegant mug. I'm sure it's not what you are used to!"

She laughed, and he dismissed her with a curt nod.

I said, "You were, then, aware of his reputation at the time, as a bent cop."

He snorted, smelled the coffee, and sipped. "Reputation!" he said, setting down the mug again. "It was a given. We all knew it and took it for granted. You couldn't get anything done in that neighborhood without going through Harragan. He ruled the roost."

"Did you have to go through him to get your practice established?"

"No! Certainly not. He knew better than to try anything with me."

I nodded. "Again, that is what I thought you would say. You have, as you say, a reputation in the neighborhood as a champion of the people, and in particular the people of the Latin-American community."

He sipped his coffee again and seemed to enjoy it. "Naturally."

I scratched my chin. "Which is why I was surprised when I came across this photograph." I took it from the folder in front of me and slipped it across the table. It was the picture that Pauli had shown us, where Ed had his arm around Rosario, and Harragan was there in his barbeque clothes.

He stared at it for a long while. He started to speak several times, but each time seemed to swallow the words before he spoke them. Finally, I said, "This was before you moved, right? That is your house."

He nodded and finally said, "I had no recollection. I don't know why he's there. Perhaps somebody else . . ."

I allowed my eyebrows to float up on my skepticism. "Matt . . . ? Sue . . . ?" I gave him a moment. When he looked up at me, I smiled and added, "Rosario . . . ?"

He reached for his coffee and took a long pull. After he'd set the mug down, he said, "I don't recall."

Dehan gave a little cough. "Were you aware, Mr. Irizarry, that

Mick Harragan was the detective in charge of investigating Rosario's rape and murder?"

"I may have been, I don't remember. It was a long time ago. I know that neighborhood was on his beat."

She reached out and took his mug. She peered inside it. "You've practically finished. I'll get you another one."

He watched her leave the room with hunted, haunted eyes, aware something was wrong but not sure what. I enlightened him.

"Were you aware, Mr. Irizarry, that semen was recovered from Rosario's body, and the lab ran a DNA test on that semen?" He went ashen. I went on. "No match was found on the database, but Harragan never took swabs from any of the people in her social circle, any of the men close to her. What do you think we will find, Mr. Irizarry, when we compare that profile with the DNA in the saliva on that mug?"

His hands were trembling and his breathing had become erratic. "You can't. It doesn't prove anything . . ."

"Why don't you tell me, Counselor, about your relationship with Rosario Rojas?"

Again he seemed unable to speak. Finally, he shook his head. "This interview is over. You have framed and manipulated me. You have acted in bad faith and cornered me when I was trying to cooperate. You have stolen my DNA. It will be declared inadmissible."

He went to stand, but his legs were trembling so bad he had to support himself on the table with his hands.

"You know that's not true, Eduardo. You know that DNA is going to tie you to Rosario's murder, and the best thing you can do is start cooperating with us right now. Tell me what happened."

He scowled at me and for a moment he looked like his old, cantankerous self. "If you are not going to charge me, this interview is over! Any further communication with me or my family will be through my attorney!"

The door opened and Dehan came in. He barreled toward her on unsteady legs, and she held the door open for him to leave. She let it swing closed after him and looked at me. I pointed.

"That is what a guilty man looks like."

She came and rested her ass on the table, looking down at me in the chair. "But guilty of what?"

I nodded. "That is the big question."

"The mug is on its way to the lab. The boots should be there by now . . ."

I raised my thumb. "Jack is eliminated as a suspect. In any case, he had no motive. Akachukwu has an alibi, but in any case had no motive. Ed looks as guilty as hell, is probably guilty of raping and murdering Rosario, *but has no motive for killing Sebastian!*" I stood and paced the room. "Dehan, we are looking at this the wrong way. We are looking at it the wrong way and that is why we cannot see the motive."

"So what is the right way, Stone?"

As she said it, her cell began to ring, and the first glimmering of light began to filter into my brain.

Then she said, "Angela! Hi . . . ! He is? That is good news. Where . . . ? We'll be there in half an hour." She hung up. "Moses. Edgewater Park. Prentiss Avenue. She's there with him now."

"Let's go."

It wasn't a long drive. We took the Bruckner Expressway and merged onto the Cross Bronx, came off onto 177th Street, then crossed the Pennyfield Avenue Bridge into Edgewater Park. It was late afternoon, edging toward evening by the time we got there, and the shadows of the old, gabled houses were stretched long across the warm blacktop. Prentiss Avenue was a short road by New York standards, and was populated by an odd assortment of ancient pine trees and ramshackle houses, and some new redbrick constructions. Others, like the one Angela had called us to, were older, faded, with paint peeling off the clapboard facades.

I parked and we climbed out into the gathering dusk. An outside staircase climbed the side of the cream-and-gray building up to a faded, weather-beaten door. Dehan climbed the stairs ahead of me and rang the bell. We saw a figure indistinctly in the window for a moment, and a couple of seconds later, the door opened, and Angela stood looking at us. She didn't say anything, but stepped back to let us in.

The place had all the feel of a fisherman's cottage. The ceiling was low and wooden, the furniture ancient and threadbare. There was an iron wood-burner in the corner, and a small propane cooker. Moses was standing in the middle of the floor, watching us. He was big, strongly built, with big hands and big feet, and a big head on a powerful neck and shoulders.

Angela stepped nervously ahead of us and gestured at him. "Detectives, this is my husband, Moses. Mo, honey, these are Detectives Stone and Dehan. They're going to help us." He studied us a moment longer, then stepped forward and held out his hand to Dehan.

"Ma'am." They shook. Then he shook my hand too. "Sir, won't you please sit down? We can't offer you much in the way of refreshment, but we have coffee."

I shook my head. "We'd be very grateful to get started on this interview, Moses." We all sat. Before I could ask him anything, he said, "I have to tell you that I am skeptical about what you say you're going to do. I am not inclined to trust the police."

Dehan answered. "I understand that, Moses. I'm sure Angela has told you that I might well have had the same feelings at one time. I hope we can change your mind. You want to tell us what's going down between you and Akachukwu Oni?"

He took a moment to think. "Ours is not such a bad neighborhood, Detectives. There are others that are much worse. It was bad at one time, but over the years it has improved. There are good people and good families living there. All over the Bronx you can see this change coming." He shook his head. "People don't want crime anymore. People are tired of living in fear."

Angela reached out and took his hand. He went on.

"It was maybe two weeks ago, nearly three. I was coming

home from work. Me and Angela have been talking about having children, making a family. I know all the families in my neighborhood, and all the kids. And I see this man, a big man, dangerous looking. He is with a couple of his friends, sitting on his car. It was a black BMW. New. And he is selling dope to some stupid young kids who are coming up to buy it from him."

He stopped and looked at me a long while, then turned to Dehan. "Why are the cops allowing this man to do this, in broad daylight, in the middle of the street? I approached him, and I heard him telling these kids, maybe sixteen or seventeen years old, that if they wanted crack, or *anything* else, he could get it for them. So I told the kids to get out of there, to go home, and that I was going to tell their parents about what they were doing. And him, I told him to get the hell out of my neighborhood, or I would put him and his friends in the hospital."

Dehan made a face. "That was a very dangerous thing to do."

"If there had been cops walking a beat there, I would not have needed to take that risk. Anyway, he told me to get lost and stay out of his way. I told him it was he and his friends who were in my way. It was they who should get lost. He took a swing at me. I was in the Marines, Detectives, and I still train regularly at the dojo. He is a big man, very tough, but the Good Lord was with me and I laid him out on his back, so he couldn't get to his feet again. His friends didn't fancy their chances with me. They just picked him up and put him in their car. But before they drove away, he pointed at me and said, 'I am going to come back, and I am going to kill you.' Just like that."

I took Akachukwu's mug shot from my wallet and showed it to him. "Is this the man?"

He nodded. "That's him."

"Did he say anything else to you?"

"Yes, sir. He said plenty. He said if I didn't like what he was doing then I should take my family and leave, because he was making a claim on that territory, and in time he was going to control Hunts Point and all the territory east of the river. I told him he could do as he pleased, but not in my neighborhood."

I glanced at Dehan. "The territory east of the river, that could include Jack's neighborhood."

"It could. It's feasible."

I turned back to Moses. "Please go on."

"So about a few days later, we are sitting having our dinner, and there is a ring at the doorbell. I go to answer it, and it is this man, and he has a gun stuck in my face. And it just flashed into my mind that it could have been Angela who opened the door. Or if God blessed us with a child, there could be a baby in that house right then. And I felt a terrible, righteous anger in that moment. I pushed the gun to one side and I hit him very hard in the face. He staggered back and fell down the stairs. May God forgive me, I prayed in that moment that the Lord should see fit to take that man's life. But he did not. I slammed the door shut, to protect Angela. But from where he was lying there on the sidewalk, he fired twice through the door. One of the shots missed and hit the wall, the other struck my leg.

"That was when I decided I must find somewhere else to live, until such time as I can afford to get Angela out of there. It never occurred to me that he would go after her too. But it seems he did. It is hard, sometimes, Detectives, to know what is the right thing to do."

Dehan sighed. "However skeptical you are of the police, Moses, once shots were fired, he attempted to murder you, you should have reported that."

He smiled at her. It was a sad smile. "I did, Detective. But no action was taken."

I glanced at Dehan. "Those slugs must be on file. Call Joe, get him to run a comparison with the slugs taken from Sebastian and Luis."

She stood, grabbed her cell, and stepped outside. Moses was watching me with humor in his eyes. When he spoke, it was without reproach, but with irony. "If I had been a young doctor, or the son of an attorney, do you think maybe the cops would have listened to me?"

I smiled back. "We are doing our best, Moses. I promise." I frowned. "Besides, I am having some trouble here, because I can't see any reason why Akachukwu Oni should go after Sebastian and Luis."

Moses spread his hands, like the answer was obvious. "The visibility was bad. He thought it was me and Angela in the car."

I nodded, then shook my head. "That's what I thought at first, but there are a couple of problems with that. First, that might make sense at six in the evening, maybe even ten at night. But who goes at three in the morning to sit outside somebody's house waiting for them to come home? Especially a couple like yourselves, who are not exactly party animals."

He made a face and nodded.

I went on. "The other thing is, he knew you'd gone. He told Angela. That's why he went to beat her up. He knew you weren't there. So what was he doing there that night at three a.m.?"

# EIGHTEEN

Dehan came back in, slipping her phone back in her jacket pocket. "He's on it."

I nodded and looked back at Moses and Angela, holding hands and watching us, waiting for us to give them a solution.

"Can you stay here?"

"This belongs to my uncle. It is not comfortable. It is not a home. But we can stay here as long as we need to."

"Then stay. You have been very lucky, Moses. Both of you have. You may not think so, but I have seen what Akachukwu is capable of, with my own eyes. So has Detective Dehan. And believe me when I tell you, you have been lucky. Stay here. Do not go back to your house until this man is convicted and in prison."

"Okay, we agree."

"Will you testify against this man at trial?"

They both nodded. "Yes, we will."

I stood. "You have both been more helpful than you can realize. We'll be in touch very soon."

Moses stood. "Detective, I have heard from friends that you have already arrested this man, and he is in prison."

"Pending trial, Moses. Don't risk it. A smart lawyer could get him bail. Stay away. Stay out of sight."

He heaved a big, reluctant sigh. "Very well."

They saw us to the door. Dusk had faded and it was now turning to evening. Streetlamps were coming on, and along the street, the warm glow of lighted windows touched the shadows of the trees and the lawns with warmth. Angela waved and closed the door, and we climbed into the Jaguar and sat staring through the windshield at the gathering darkness.

Dehan gazed at me. After a while, it dawned on me that I was gazing back, and it struck me suddenly how absurd and intimate it was that we were sitting in a dark car in a dark street, just gazing at each other without talking. I blinked and sighed.

"So now, what I want to do, Dehan, is eliminate Akachukwu Oni from Sebastian's murder inquiry."

"What?"

"I want to send him down for Jack's murder and for the attempts on Moses and Angela . . ."

"You think he killed Jack?"

"I'm certain of it."

"But you don't think he killed Sebastian . . ."

"No. But we need to prove that."

"You are going to have two problems there, Stone. One, you're trying to prove a negative, and two, I think he did kill him."

I shook my head. "I don't see either of those as a problem, but tell me what his motive is for killing Sebastian."

"He hasn't got one."

I smiled. "Okay . . ."

"He wasn't there waiting for the car. He arrived with the intention of breaking in and finding out from Angela where Moses was. But when he arrived, he saw the car wasn't there. So he waited. Maybe he thought he'd wait for her to return, or maybe he was just wondering what to do. Either way, he didn't have to wait long, because the car turned up. In the poor visibility, he saw two people but couldn't make out exactly who they were. Naturally, he assumed it was Moses and Angela. Being how he is, he didn't hesitate. He got out, walked up, and emptied his magazine. Then drove away."

I drummed on the wheel with my fingers for a moment. "It's possible."

"But you don't buy it."

I sighed. "I am hungry, tired, and thirsty. Let's call it a day and see how it looks in the morning. Forensics will make things a bit clearer."

I followed Ellsworth Avenue and, at the bridge, without thinking, I turned onto East Tremont, headed north. We didn't talk. I'd noticed she'd been odd for the last couple of days. I had half assumed it was her time of the month, or something equally incomprehensible to men, and guessed it would pass in time. I didn't give it a lot of thought. I'd had a crazy idea. I had no evidence as yet, but hard as I tried to pick holes in it, I couldn't. It worked, and that's probably why, when we came to Westchester, I continued north on Williamsbridge Road, instead of turning west onto East Tremont; probably why I didn't take the Bruckner Expressway in the first place; probably why it never even crossed my mind to ask her what she wanted to do.

Now she looked at me with that same expressionless face she'd had for the past couple of days and said, "What are you doing, Stone?"

I gave her a blank look back. "What?"

"Where are you going?"

"Home."

She blinked a couple of times. "I have to get a cab?"

I smiled, then laughed. "Sorry, Dehan! I should have asked. I thought we could have those bison steaks and a bottle of wine. It might stimulate the little gray cells. What do you say?"

She didn't smile or laugh. She looked away from me, out of the window, and after a moment, she said, "Just drop me on Morris Park Avenue. I'll get a cab. Thanks all the same."

I felt a flush of anger start in my belly and rise up to my head. I stayed quiet until it passed. I didn't drop her at Morris Park

Avenue. She turned and looked at me as I crossed over it and kept watching me as I turned into Rhinelander and eventually Haight Avenue, and parked in front of my house. There, I killed the engine and turned in my seat to face her.

"Dehan, I can cook you a bison steak on the barbeque, I can help you cook a bison steak on the barbeque, or I can drive you home. I am not, after a year of considering you more than a partner, more than a friend . . ." I was momentarily lost for words. ". . . considering you *family*! I am not going to drop you on Morris Park Avenue to get a cab. And frankly, I feel insulted that you would expect me to."

She looked down at her hands in her lap. I waited, but she didn't say anything, so I asked her, "Dehan, ever since we got back from Goa you've been . . ." Again I was lost for words. Now she raised her eyes and watched me.

She said, "What?"

I gestured at her. "Like this! Talk to me! Tell me what's going on!"

She looked strangely sad. "Nothing's going on, Stone."

I shook my head. "That's not true. Something happened in Goa. As I recall, we had a great time. Then, on the last day, you started to . . ." I searched for the word. I noticed her smile, but it was a smile of sad irony. I frowned, said again, "You started to go like this. What happened in Goa, Dehan?"

She reached over and took my hand, gave it a small squeeze. "Nothing." She gave the word an odd emphasis. "Nothing happened in Goa." She gave a small laugh and patted my hand. "You're a great detective, Mr. Stone, but I guess there are some things you just can't work out. Enjoy your steak. I'll see you in the morning."

She climbed out of the car, and I sat confused, watching her tall, elegant form, on those long, extraordinary legs, walk away from me. As she passed through the dappled glow of a streetlamp, under a plane tree, she reached behind her head and tied her long, black hair into a knot. I felt a sharp pang of loss. I got out of the car and drew breath to shout after her. But she passed out of the glow, into the shadows, and soon after that, she turned onto Rhinelander Avenue and I saw her raise her hand to hail a cab. I had been too slow, and now it was too late.

I sat on the hood of my Jag, staring at the empty glow of the avenue at the end of the gloomy tunnel which was my street. My mind was still and quiet. It seemed to be empty of thought, but I heard myself mutter, "What happened in Goa . . . ?"

*Nothing happened in Goa.*

I climbed the stairs to my house, let myself in, and poured myself a whiskey.

# NINETEEN

THE CALL CAME A LITTLE AFTER TWO A.M. I WAS STILL up, sitting in my chair with a third glass of whiskey in my hand, staring at the cold, empty fireplace. The ringing roused me from dark thoughts and memories. I reached for my phone and saw it was Frank.

"Yeah! Hi . . ."

"Sorry to wake you, John, I thought you'd want to know. I'm here with Joe, all the results are in . . ."

"No. I was up. I'll come right over."

"You were up?" He sounded curious.

"Yeah, long story. See you in ten minutes."

It was just half a mile from my house to the Van Etten Building, and at that time there was no traffic, so I made it in less than ten minutes. I found them both in Frank's small office, drinking coffee laced with whiskey out of paper cups. I'd had an idea that's what they'd be doing, so I put my contribution of half a bottle of Irish on the table and pulled up a chair.

"What have you got?"

Joe poured me some coffee, laced it, and handed it to me.

"First of all, the boot prints at the scene of Jack O'Brien's murder: they were made by the boots you had sent in, which places your man Akachukwu at the scene of the murder, removing the cannabis plants."

I nodded. "That's good."

"Yeah, but there is more. What we hadn't spotted on the first, cursory glance, was that there was blood on the boots, on the soles and on the uppers. The blood is in the prints he left behind, in the dust, and still in the stitching and the overlaps of the boots. Naturally, the blood is a match for O'Brien. Those boots were not only at the scene of the murder, removing the cannabis, they were there at the *time* of the murder, removing the cannabis."

"That is damn good work, Joe."

Frank sipped and said, "I can confirm what we already assumed, that he was killed by a single slash of an extremely sharp blade. Something like a samurai sword or a razor-sharp machete. He was then beaten, probably kicked, and his spine broken, but that occurred postmortem."

I took a swig. "Poor bastard."

Frank nodded. "Not the nicest way to go. Now, to make your life a little more complicated, the DNA you sent in on the mug, it was a match for the DNA found in Rosario Rojas. Whoever drank from that cup, also raped Rosario."

I gave an unhappy laugh. "So both are almost certainly guilty of a crime which is *not* killing Sebastian Acosta."

They both grunted and we all drank.

"Logic dictates that one of the two was there that night."

Joe leaned down into his bag and extracted a folder. He dropped it in front of me. "There are all your results. I don't know if it helps, but the slugs that were removed from Sebastian, Luis, and the car are not a match for the slugs that were removed from Angela's hall and Moses' leg. Those two were forty-fives. Moses was lucky that slug had traveled through a door before it hit him. It might have done a hell of a lot more damage otherwise.

"The slugs that killed Sebastian and injured Luis were thirty-eights." He shrugged. "Doesn't mean they weren't fired by the same man, it just means they came out of a different gun."

I sat tipping my coffee one way and another. "If you wanted to kill somebody, as a punishment, not for expediency, but to bolster your reputation as a badass, and you owned a forty-five, would you use your thirty-eight for the job?"

Joe shook his head. "I'd take the biggest, baddest gun I had."

Frank nodded. "And I have to tell you, what whoever it was did to Sebastian is what they used to call a cowboy. That was back in the days of Dutch Schultz and Bumpy Johnson. If you did a cowboy on somebody, you shot them dead and you just kept shooting until you'd emptied the magazine. You weren't just killing them, you were destroying them, and their reputation."

I nodded several times. Joe topped up my cup, so it was now whiskey stained with coffee. "At least you'll have enough for a search warrant. You may find the cannabis plants. You'll have trouble making anything stick with Irizarry, though. He'll claim they had consensual sex, and proving he strangled her is going to be hard. The prints they lifted back then were no good. It'll be down to the DA persuading the jury."

I frowned. "How about the prints on Angela's neck? You get anything there?"

He shook his head. "He was wearing gloves."

I shrugged. "That's not a problem. When the jury hears about Jack, they hear Moses' and Angela's testimony, and me and Dehan swear we saw him there moments after she was attacked, they'll know what conclusion to come to."

They both nodded, then they both frowned. It was Frank who voiced it, though.

"Say, what gives with you and Dehan?"

I raised an eyebrow. "This again?"

"Come on, John. How many years have we known each other? This isn't idle gossip, we are concerned about you. You don't seem yourself."

I didn't know what to say, so I took another swig of whiskey. Joe was studying me. He glanced at Frank. "To be honest, John, when you went to Goa, we thought you were going to come back . . ." He shrugged. "At the very least happy! We expected, well . . ."

I sighed. "You're not alone, the whole damned precinct seems to have been thinking the same thing. What's the big deal?"

Frank shook his head. "Don't misread it, John. You may not realize it, but you are well liked and well respected; people wish you well. Dehan also. She had a lot of attitude when she arrived, but she's mellowed a lot since you two were partnered. She's a damned fine cop and . . ." He stopped and glanced at Joe, who shrugged.

I said, "What?"

It was Joe who answered. "Well, John, everybody except you seems to have noticed that she . . ." He sighed, then laughed. "God knows why, but she is serious about you." He glanced at Frank. "And we think she's good for you."

I stared at them both. "Who is 'we'?"

They both spoke in unison, like some surreal sitcom. "Everybody."

We drank some more, had a bit more "guys" talk—I do not recall what I said or what I admitted to—but at almost four a.m., I walked out of the Van Etten Building with my hands in my pockets, thinking deeply and humming Sinatra's "One for my Baby (and One More for the Road)."

I climbed into my car and sat for five minutes staring out the windshield at the empty, lamplit streets. I pulled out my phone, opened WhatsApp, and stared at her name for another five minutes. Then I opened our conversation. We were cops. We had no fixed sleeping hours. We sent each other important information at any time. That was how it was. That was what I told myself.

I looked at my watch. It was gone four. I wondered if I was drunk and decided I was, a little.

I typed: *Boot-print confirmed. DNA Ed Irizarry. Bullets not a match. Crime scene .38, door .45*

I pressed Send, put the phone away, and fired up the engine.

There was an immediate ping. I left the car in neutral and looked at my phone. It was Dehan. I opened the message.

*Shit. No closer to an answer then.*

I stared at it for a long moment. Then wrote, *I am not sure. I think so.* Then, *You're awake?*

I sent it and waited. There was no reply. I put the car in gear and moved to the gate. As I was about to pull onto Morris Park and head home, there was another ping. I stopped, selected neutral again, and pulled out my phone. It was a reply from Dehan.

*You feel like an early breakfast? I can scramble some eggs.*

I sat motionless for a long moment. There was another ping. *You there?*

I typed: *Yes. Your place?*

*That'd be a first.*

*We could try something new.*

Silence.

I put the car in gear, ready to go home. Another ping. I put it back in neutral, read the message.

*We could do that.*

I typed, *I'm on my way.*

Fifteen minutes later, I parked outside her block. I sat for a couple of minutes, conscious that my breath probably smelled of booze. I told myself not to be an ass, then climbed out, crossed the road, and rang on her bell. She let me in almost immediately, and when I reached her floor she was standing there, with the door open, dressed in a pair of shorts and a T-shirt.

I smiled. "You couldn't sleep either, huh?"

She shook her head. "You came empty-handed."

"Good job you have tequila."

She smiled. "You been drinking, Sensei?"

"It's what guys do."

She gave a small laugh. "Does that make me a guy?"

I waited a moment, then said, "I hope not."

She turned and went inside. "You've only been here once."

"I remember. I won't forget in a hurry."

"Neither will I."

She closed the door. I was in the living room. She had a bottle of tequila on her coffee table, and a shot glass beside it. The bottle was half empty. She had Stan Getz playing.

I turned to look at her. "You like Stan Getz?"

"Yeah. He's very cool. You mentioned him once, so I decided to explore. Miles too, when he's not drilling teeth. You want some scrambled eggs and bacon?"

"Yes."

She went into the kitchen. "So, how'd it go?"

I leaned on the doorjamb and watched her break and beat eggs. "Frank and Joe had a bottle and some coffee on the go. They called me at just after two."

"Were you in bed?"

"No. So I drove over. I told you the results in the WhatsApp. I think . . ."

She turned and came over to me. She put her right hand on my chest and looked up at me with large, black eyes.

"Let's try something different."

I shut my mouth and frowned. "Okay."

"We eat, we drink tequila, and we talk about anything—*anything*—ancient Egypt, reincarnation, Donald Trump, baseball, Elon Musk; you name it, anything but work."

I nodded. "Okay."

She shrugged and made a Latin face. "And then we see what happens."

What happened was that we talked and we got drunk, and then we talked some more and we got drunk some more, and it was one of the most enjoyable evenings I had had in years; maybe ever. I told her about my parents, about my wife, about life as a bachelor cop. She told me more about her parents, about her dad's family and her mother's, and about life as a single, female cop. We talked about movies we liked and music we loved, books, poems, peculiar memories . . .

And we laughed a lot. And a couple of times, while she laughed, she leaned on my shoulder. It was astonishing to discover, after a year of working so closely together, how many things we did not know about each other, and how much we shared in common. It was good.

At six a.m., she looked at her watch and said, "Hooooly shshshsh . . ." Then she gave me a long, steady look. It was a drunk look, but it was a steady look too. "I was going to ask you if you wanted the couch . . . or not . . . But it is time for a cold shower, Mr. Stone, and a gallon of coffee. We have work to do. Make coffee! I am going to shower."

She walked unsteadily into the bedroom. I shook my head, took a few deep breaths, and went into the kitchen wondering if I had heard right, and if so, what the hell I was going to do about it.

# TWENTY

At nine a.m., Akachukwu was brought into interview room three and manacled to the table again.

I asked him, "Do you wish to have an attorney present?"

He shook his head. "Not right now, no. If I change my mind, I will let you know."

"Mr. Oni, I have to inform you that we are charging you with the murder of Mr. Jack O'Brien, as well as the assault on Angela Rojas, the attempted murder of Moses Johnson and Luis Irizarry, and the murder of Sebastian Acosta. Do you still say you do not want to have an attorney present?"

He smiled. "It seems I have been a busy man. I will hear what you have to say, and then I will decide whether I want an attorney or not."

I shrugged. I was about to speak, but Dehan interrupted me. "Excuse me, Detective Stone, just a quick question. Mr. Oni, have you lent any of your clothing to anybody in the last few days?"

He laughed and shook his head. "No, Detective, I have not. But let me assure you that it is not difficult to find a black sweater and a ski mask in New York!"

She smiled. "Thank you, Mr. Oni, that's good to know."

I smiled too. "How about size thirteen boots?"

"They are also readily available, Detective, if you are that well endowed."

Dehan smiled. "You don't know anybody that well endowed?"

"I do not. Do you?"

"So you haven't lent your boots to anyone."

He laughed. "I don't know anybody whose . . . *feet* are that big."

I gave him a moment, then said, "Mr. Oni, we have given you three opportunities to deny it, but it is clear that you have not lent your boots to anybody in the last few days." Now he frowned, but I went on. "Your boots were used yesterday in the murder of Jack O'Brien at his home in Hunt Avenue, and also in the theft of at least twelve cannabis plants from the same address. The unique tread of those boots was found at his home, and his blood was also found in those prints and in the boots themselves. What have you to say to that, Mr. Oni?"

His eyes remained dead and unexpressive. "I have no comment to make at this time."

I nodded. "We also have testimony from Moses Johnson that you threatened to kill him because he struck you in self-defense when he found you selling drugs in his neighborhood. You were at the time being driven by two associates in a black BMW. What do you say to that, Mr. Oni?"

He shook his head. "I have no comment to make at this time."

"Very well. Mr. Johnson also states that a few days later you came to his house and threatened him with a gun. He knocked you down the stairs and you fired two forty-five caliber bullets through his door. One struck the wall and the other struck him in the leg. Both of these bullets have been recovered. Have you any comment to make about that?"

"Like I said, I have no comment to make at this time."

"It is our belief that you later returned to Angela Rojas' house and assaulted her in an attempt to find out where Moses Johnson was, because you intended to kill him. Have you any comment to make about that?"

He shook his head. "No comment."

Dehan slammed her open hand down on the table. It made a loud noise that echoed in the small room. "Seriously? Is that all you've got? *No comment?* How about this, Akachukwu? Moses, who is a *real* man, who incidentally also has big feet, humiliated you in front of your goons and in front of the whole damn street! Your little ego is so fragile that you could not take that humiliation, and all you could think to do, in your ignorant *little* mind, was to kill him! Because anybody who stands up to pathetic, little Ak Oni must be destroyed! In case they reveal sad, pathetic, little Ak Oni for what he really is: an ignorant, stupid, impotent *little* coward!"

She stood up and leaned across the table at him. His eyes were hooded, and you could see death in them. Dehan didn't seem to notice. Or if she did, she didn't care.

"So you went after him, not with your hands, not in an equal, man-to-man fight. Because you're *not* a man! Because *you* are too damn chickenshit to face him man to man! You went after him with a gun. And even with a gun in your hand, he *still* knocked you down!"

She walked around the table and stood behind him. His face was impassive, but I could see his breathing had got faster and shallower. She kept on, relentless and mocking.

"So what did the big, dangerous, scary, *terrifying* Ak Oni do then? Because he was too damned chickenshit to go after Moses, he went after his *girlfriend*." She laughed out loud. "But even *she* made you run!" He opened his mouth, but then shut it again. "You weren't even man enough to make *her* talk. She screamed and fought back like a wildcat, and you ran."

She came around the table and stood looking down at his face. It was expressionless, but it radiated contempt. He watched her with half-closed eyes. She pushed some more.

"I guess you lost a lot of sleep over how small, how weak and pathetic they both made you look, huh, Akachukwu? Till one night you couldn't handle it anymore and you went over there. You told your girlfriends to start without you. Got them to lie for you. I guess you get that a lot, huh? Girls lying for you, so you can save face. 'Oh, you're amazing, Ak. Oh, you're a *real* man, Ak! Oh, Ak, you're such an *animal*!'" She snorted. "You waited outside Angela's house, trying to build up enough courage to go in and face her again. Then the car pulled up, and like the coward that you are, you got out, went over, and shot through the window, without even checking to see who it was inside."

There was a long moment of heavy silence while he gazed at his manacles. Finally, he shook his head and smiled. It was a thin, sickly smile, with something oddly terrifying about it. "That is a fascinating story, Detective Dehan." He raised his eyes to look at her. "*Carmen*, in spite of all the insults and the abuse, and the attempts to intimidate me and force a false confession out of me. But I can tell you that it is all a fabrication, an intellectual construct of your own, and none of it is true. On that night that you are alluding to, I was in bed with my three favorite girlfriends, and they will corroborate that in court, as you well know."

He turned his eyes on me. "I may have been at the house on Hunt Avenue, I do not remember very clearly, and I may have gone to visit Angela, in the spirit of a good neighbor, to see if she was okay, but I did not kill Jack O'Brien. I cannot explain how that blood got on my boots. And I was not at Angela's house on the night that those boys were so tragically killed." He shrugged again and smiled. "My house was full of people. I am a very generous friend and neighbor, I can produce many witnesses if necessary, to vouch for my whereabouts on that night."

I nodded. "No doubt, Mr. Oni, but your boots place you firmly at Jack O'Brien's house, killing him and stealing his cannabis. Tell me something, did you use a samurai sword or a machete?"

"I have no comment to make on that score at the present time."

I studied his face carefully. "I have acquired a search warrant for your house, and there is a CSI team on their way there now. What do you think they'll find?"

His eyes glazed and his lids lowered.

I went on. "Will they find the cannabis plants, with Jack O'Brien's prints on the pots? Will they find a machete?" I gave a small laugh. "You didn't reckon on the boot prints, did you? You didn't realize they could be as distinctive as fingerprints."

"I have cooperated with you, Detectives, and all I have got in return is abuse and insults, and your latent racial denigration. I will cooperate no more. I think it is time for me to have my attorney now."

I nodded and stood. "I think you are probably right, Mr. Oni. You'd better give him a call."

Dehan stood too, and leaned across the table at him again. "And my advice, Ak, start thinking about *really* cooperating, for real, because the jury is not going to like you. I can guarantee that."

We stepped out of the room and told the uniforms outside to take him back to his cell. As we watched him led away, Dehan cussed under her breath. "He's as cool as he is stupid."

I smiled and nodded. "Fortunately for us, Little Grasshopper, he is one of those people who thinks the more elaborately they talk, the more their IQ score goes up. He really believes he's smart." I glanced at her. She looked the way I felt, a little pasty and green around the edges. "How are you holding up?"

"Okay. I could use some more coffee."

I nodded. Coffee sounded good, but before I could suggest it, my phone rang. I pulled it from my pocket.

"Yeah, Stone."

"Detective Stone, this is Dr. Delgado at the Jacobi. Luis Irizarry has regained consciousness. He is able to talk to you for a short while, but I must insist that you do not tax him or upset him. He is still very weak."

"You got it, Doc. We're on our way." I hung up.

Dehan shrugged and made a question with her face. I said, "Luis. He's conscious. Let's go!"

———

HE WAS SITTING UP. His skin was sallow, and his eyes were yellow where they should have been white. He was connected to a drip, and a heart monitor was bleeping quietly in the background. Mary was sitting on the far side of the bed in an armchair, holding his hand, gazing at him. Ed was on a straight-backed chair next to her, scowling at me and Dehan.

The door swung closed behind us. Ed stood. The last time I'd seen him he'd been trembling. He was still trembling now. I wondered absently if he'd been trembling the whole time in between.

"What are you doing here?"

"The doctor called us. We'd like to ask Luis a couple of questions. We'll keep it short and sweet."

"Out of the question! How dare you . . . !"

Mary and Luis spoke almost in unison. "Dad . . ."

"Eduardo . . ."

He looked at them both in turn. Luis said, "Can you please just not . . . ?"

He glared at me. "Very well, but the minute you upset him, you are out of here."

I didn't answer. I pulled up a straight-backed chair and sat by Luis' side. Dehan sat on the foot of the bed and smiled at him. He smiled back.

"My name is John Stone. This here is Carmen Dehan. We're detectives with the Forty-Third Precinct." I smiled. "Welcome back."

He gave a lopsided grin. "Yeah, thanks. I still feel pretty weak."

"I bet you do, but before long, you'll be back on your feet again. Luis, we'd like to catch whoever did this to you."

He gave a small laugh. "Yeah, me too."

Dehan grinned. "That's the spirit. But listen, if it's hard or upsetting, we can come back some other time."

He shook his head. "No, I'm okay. The fact is I don't remember much." His eyes drifted just past Dehan's right shoulder, like he could see there the events of that night playing themselves out again. He took a deep breath. "We went in Angela's car to get some beer. We stopped at the ATM, then we went to the twenty-four seven store. We got some cans. I remember I wanted to get a bottle of vodka, but Seb said no, Angela wouldn't like that. Then we came back . . ." He looked at me and frowned. "We'd parked out front of the house. Seb killed the engine and the lights. But there was a car ahead of us. He had his lights on high beam. It was blinding. I remember a figure. It was hard to make out because he was kind of backlit, you know what I mean?" I nodded. He went on, "He was standing with the headlamps behind him, so he was sort of like a hazy silhouette. I remember Seb said, 'What the hell does this joker want?' Then he came up to Seb's window . . ." He shook his head. "And that's all I remember."

I heard Dehan repress a sigh. "You didn't see his face?"

He shook his head.

I said, "You're doing great, Luis, and we are nearly done. You said that the image was like a hazy silhouette. Could you make out what sort of size he was?" I grinned. "Assuming he was more than five foot and less than seven, where would you place him in between?"

He thought about it. In the background I heard the rate of the heart monitor accelerate slightly. Finally, he took a deep breath. "I'm sorry I can't be more helpful, Detective. I'd say he was more than average. But aside from that, I don't seem to have retained any more details."

I shook my head. "Not at all, Luis, you've been very helpful. Maybe when you're stronger we can have another try."

I saw his eyes shift to look past me at the door. I heard it open, and Dehan and I both turned to look. I heard Ed splutter, "What the hell is this?"

Moses and Angela were standing in the doorway, and behind them was Sue.

Ed took a step toward them and snarled, "What do you mean by coming here to my son's room?"

Luis sighed and looked away, closing his eyes. Mary rose and placed a hand on Ed's sleeve. He yanked his arm away, ignoring her, speaking to Angela and Sue. "Get out of here . . . !"

I stood, and Dehan stood with me. I said, "Mr. Irizarry, could I have a word with you outside?"

Then several things happened all at once: Mary hurried around him, saying, "Sue! Angela! It is so nice of you to have come!" Sue and Mary embraced, and Angela moved toward the bed, holding out her hands to Luis.

Luis reached out for her. "Angie, I am so sorry!"

Ed was looking this way and that, like a man losing control, his face flushed with anger. I stepped over close to him and spoke quietly. "Let's try to do this without upsetting your son. Step outside with me or I will cuff you right here."

He stared into my face like he wanted to shoot me where I stood, there and then. Dehan came up close by his side and we moved to the door as Mary, Sue, and Moses moved toward the bed. Out in the corridor, Ed started in on me. "What is the *meaning* of this? How *dare* you come to . . ."

I cut him short. "Can it. We got the results on your DNA from the mug. Ed Irizarry, I am putting you under arrest for the rape and murder of Rosario Rojas."

# TWENTY-ONE

HE BURIED HIS FACE IN HIS HANDS AND TURNED AWAY from me, saying, "No, no, no, you've got it all wrong. This can't be happening . . . !" He looked strangely infantile, but at the same time it seemed fitting in a man who had lived his life as a series of childish tantrums.

"It's happening, Ed. And you know yourself that the best thing you can do now is cooperate with us and tell us the truth."

He turned fiercely to face me. "What is *wrong* with you? I did not kill her! Why would I kill her? Are you insane?"

An orderly walked past and glanced at us but kept going on her way. Protocol said I should cuff him and take him in. My gut said I should keep him talking. My gut wins every time. I said, "Because you raped her. And if you'd let her live, she would have reported you to the cops and that would have been the end of your career as the great man of the people."

He spat savagely, "*You're out of your mind! You don't know anything!*"

Dehan must have had the same feeling as me, because she said, "Fine. Why don't you enlighten us?"

"I was *in love* with Rosario! Why would I kill her? I *adored* her! It almost destroyed me when she was murdered! It almost finished me, my career, everything!"

I sighed and shook my head. "Save it for the jury, Ed. That's horseshit and you know it."

"It is *not*! She was the only woman I ever truly loved! How *dare* you use that language about her! She was smart, elegant, intelligent, sensitive! She was a *real* woman!" His eyes flashed over at the door behind me in a silent comparison with his wife, who sat beyond it. "God is my witness, I was not worthy of her . . ." There was no mistaking his sincerity, and another piece in the puzzle slotted into place in my mind.

"You really were, weren't you . . ."

"Yes . . . I was, and I still am. I always will be."

Dehan's eyes were narrowed. Two and two were making five for her and she didn't like it. She said, "If you were so in love with her, why did you rape Susanne Mackenzie?"

He sneered at her. "You *stupid* woman!"

I snapped, "Watch your mouth, Counselor!"

"As if I would waste my time on that pretentious, middle-class, bleeding-heart pseudo-socialist inverted *snob*!"

"Wow . . ." He turned to stare at me, like I'd said something important. I went on, "That's some put-down. A lot of contempt."

He curled his lip. "It's what she is."

I nodded. "It's interesting. You must have read this yourself, Ed, that rape is not a sexual crime. Because the motivation is to humiliate, to humble somebody. Is that how you feel about Sue Mackenzie?"

"Don't be absurd! I don't feel anything for that woman. She is a nonentity, a hanger-on, a groupie. Why Mateo ever married her is beyond me."

Dehan said, "She is prepared to swear in court that you raped her. With the DNA evidence that you raped Rosario, that is going to be pretty compelling for a jury."

He stared at her like he wanted to slap her. Suddenly he

advanced on her, poking with his index finger, then on me, then on Dehan again, like he couldn't make up his mind which of us to tackle. "Just *think*! Let me ask you something. You think you're so damned smart, well just *think*! If I killed Rosario so she wouldn't report me to the *damned* cops, *why the hell did I not kill Susanne? You don't make any sense!*"

He had a point, and it was something I had been asking myself for a while. It was one of the things that had driven me to the conclusion I had reached. Now my gut told me I was close to getting some hard evidence.

"Okay, Ed, I'll tell you what we are going to do. We're going to go and get a coffee, and you are going to tell us the whole story, *everything*! Start bullshitting me and I will take you in and put you on trial. You understand me?"

He scowled at me resentfully. "Of course I understand you. I am not a moron."

Five minutes later, we sat around a table in the café. Dehan and I waited while he stirred two packs of sugar into a double espresso. When he was done, he made an ugly face and shrugged.

"Susanne was my wife's friend. Matt was a good man. We had been friends for a long time. We had similar ideas. He was more . . ." He made that ugly face again, that had something of contempt in it. "More idealistic. Forgive-and-forget socialism. He thought that education was the answer to everything." He shrugged, lifted his cup with his baby finger stuck out, and pursed his lips. He sipped noisily, then shrugged again, with only one shoulder. "Me, I think unforgiving litigation is the best lesson you can teach anybody. Nothing shapes society so well or so fast as litigation."

I nodded once and sighed. "Can we move on from the lesson in social engineering?"

He made a dismissive noise like, "Yah!" and carried on. "Matt and me had a lot to talk about. We used to discuss national and international politics, but more than that, we were very involved in local politics, restoring the balance of power away from . . ." He jerked his head at me. "People like you, to a more representative range of the community."

I asked him, "Did that include people like Mick Harragan?" He went quiet. "You're not on a soapbox now, Ed, and there is no jury for you to impress. I know who you are, you're a jumped-up power-grabbing politico just like the people you profess to fight against, like Harragan. Now quit playacting and tell me about your relationship with Sue and with Rosario. So far, you are just confirming my belief that you raped them, and Mick got you off the hook."

Dehan was looking antsy. She turned to me. "What are we doing here, Stone? Okay, it's a valid question, why'd he kill Rosario and not Sue? How about this? Rosario swore she'd report him to the cops, go over Mick's head and make it stick. Sue was weak and didn't want to upset the applecart. Let's get this son of a bitch down to the station, because if I have to listen to one more of his damned political speeches, I swear . . ."

He raised both his hands. "Okay, okay, okay . . ."

"Talk about a goddamn racist, misogynist . . . !"

"Okay!"

She turned to stare at him. He made placating movements with his hands.

"Okay, you made your point. Mary and Susanne were active in the community, in various ways, and they often ran into Rosario. Rosario was . . ." He shrugged. "*Different.* She was not like any woman I ever met. At first, she used to come over to visit Mary and Susanne, but her conversation, her curiosity, her hunger for knowledge and understanding . . ." He smiled and shook his head. "She was extraordinary. Matt and I started recommending books to her. She would read them and talk about them, *intelligently*! Soon Susanne and Mary's conversation became boring for her." He laughed. "She would join in with me and Matt instead." He wagged a finger at me, smiling. "She would not always agree with us! Oh no! Often she would disagree! And she would argue with that fire that only a Latina can have!" He went quiet, and the joy drained from his face. "It was not long before I realized that I was in love with her. Mary . . . pah! What was she compared with this passionate, beautiful, intelligent woman? *Nothing!*"

He sat staring at his cold, sweet coffee. "I could not keep silent. I told her. I had to tell her. I was burning inside!" He looked up at me like I would understand, and nodded several times. "She felt the same way. We had to be together." He frowned and wagged his finger again. "It could not be straight-away. I was in the middle of an important trial, which was going to establish my reputation. A divorce right then, and especially a divorce from a Puerto Rican woman, it could have undermined my position and my reputation. But we became lovers. I used to go and see her regularly at lunchtime. I helped her with her rent. We made plans." He shook his head and tears glinted in his eyes. "We were going to be married. She was going to be my wife."

He was quiet for a long moment. We waited. He took a deep breath and shrugged.

"The trial finished. We won. My reputation was secured. I went to see Rosario. I told her, 'I am going to arrange the papers, before the weekend I am going to tell Mary it's over, and when the divorce is final, we will get married.' She was so happy! We made love . . ." He shook his head, like he was having trouble counting. ". . . Two or three times. Then I went back to the office. I prepared the papers, I talked to my friend Alfredo, asked him to represent me, and when I got home, I found Mary and Susanne crying. Hugging each other. What happened? They were hysterical, but finally they tell me. Rosario has been killed. Murdered."

We were all silent. After a moment, I asked him, "What happened?"

"I passed out." He stared straight at me. "Right there, on the spot. I passed out. I lost consciousness." He snapped his fingers. "Mary knew. If she had any doubts before, right then she knew." He kept shaking his head. "You know? I made no effort to hide it. I didn't care if she realized or not. But if she missed it before, right then she knew." He sighed. "I called Mick. I told him about me and Rosario. He said he knew about it. That was why he had respected her. He liked Latina women. He would have liked to have Rosario, but he knew she was mine. So he respected her. He asked me, did I kill her? I told him of course not. He was a good man. He understood. He said that was enough for him. But they never caught the son of a bitch who did it."

Dehan stood and walked out of the café. Ed watched her leave. I said, "That good man who was such a great pal of yours?" He turned to look at me. "That corrupt gangster in a uniform, that son of a bitch raped and murdered her mother and put her father in the hospital, while she watched. She didn't kill him because he beat her so badly she couldn't move. That friend and ally of yours was a parasite on the Latino community you claim to protect and serve."

He looked away.

I went on, "So what about Susanne?"

He raised an eyebrow at me. It was like contempt was an autonomic response with him. He couldn't help it. "Nothing about Susanne. I told you, she was nothing to me. Less than that."

"So what was your problem with Sebastian?"

Before he could answer, Dehan came back. She had obviously breathed and counted to ten. I asked her with a look, and she gave me one back that said she was okay. I asked Ed again, "What was your problem with Sebastian, Ed? Because I am having trouble swallowing the line that says, Sue accuses you of raping her, at about the same time Rosario gets raped and murdered, and then Sue's son is murdered outside Rosario's house—and you have *nothing* to do with it." I shook my head. "That is hard to swallow."

He shrugged. "Hard or not, it's the truth. Sebastian? He was nothing, like his mother. Same kind of weak thinking as his father, but without the intelligence. Education will lead to equality? Look at the profession he chose! Investigating the dead! What use is that? They're dead, for crying out loud! Do something useful!"

Dehan raised an eyebrow, and her voice was acerbic to the

point of being almost venomous. "Like providing skin-deep beauty to the rich?"

She looked at me. I sighed. "Ed, don't go anywhere. Do not leave the city. I am not done with you."

"I am no longer under arrest?"

I shook my head. "But I will be looking for evidence to corroborate Susanne Mackenzie's story."

"You mean you'll be manufacturing it!"

I stood. "That was your friend and ally Mick's game, not mine."

We left him staring at his hands on the table and made our way out to the parking lot.

# TWENTY-TWO

WE WERE BACK AT EMILIO'S PIZZA JOINT. DEHAN WAS staring at her pizza like she couldn't see it. "You know," she said, "if I were like Mick, I'd put him away. I'd fabricate the damned evidence and put the son of a bitch away. Because he deserves it, because of the way he treats women, because of the way he treats *people*! The world doesn't need more bastards like Ed Irizarry. But I can't do that."

I nodded. "I know."

"You know why I can't do it?"

"Because you're a good person."

"No," she said, illogically, "I can't do it because that would make me like him! And I am *not* like him!"

I frowned but didn't ask the obvious question. I wasn't sure she was listening to me. I picked up a piece of pizza and bit into it. While I chewed, she stared out the window. After a bit, she said, "You believe him, don't you?"

I swallowed. "Do you?"

She made a sound that was almost a growl and buried her face in her hands, then ran her fingers through her hair. "Man, I really did not need a hangover today!"

I smiled. "Do you regret it?"

She looked at me sharply, then slowly smiled. "No." She flopped back in her chair. "I'm sorry I was . . . weird. It's complicated."

I raised my eyebrows and nodded.

Before I could say anything, she added, "But it's nice to be back to normal."

"Are we?"

She looked surprised.

I went on, "Were we ever?"

"I don't know what you mean."

"We were never normal, Carmen."

"I guess not."

I pulled off half my beer. "Beer is good for a hangover, Ritoo Glasshopper. We'll talk later. Right now, let us consider the state of the case."

She did several things with her eyebrows that were hard to follow, then said, "If you believe that piece of . . . If you believe Irizarry, we have a real problem. Because we have gone from having too many suspects, to not having any at all. And *somebody* murdered Sebastian."

"Of that there can be no doubt, Dehan. But we must not fall into the trap of making the facts fit our theories. If it was not Jack O'Brien, it was not Akachukwu, and it was not Ed Irizarry, then it must have been somebody else."

She spread her hands, looking at me aghast. "*Who?* There isn't anybody else!"

I shook my head, bit into another slice of pizza, and spoke with my mouth full. "Yum cum shee amybobby erf."

"I can't see anybody else."

I nodded. "Mm-hm . . ."

"Okay, Sensei, enlighten me."

I shrugged, swallowed, and drank beer. "Think. What is the eternal motivation for murder?"

"Sex."

"So who might have had reason to be sexually jealous?"

"Of Sebastian?"

"For example . . ."

"Um . . ." She looked abstracted, frowning out of the window at the bright June day. "Um . . ."

"Was he good-looking?"

"Yeah, I guess he was."

"An attractive young intern with a bright future. You think maybe Angela might have been attracted to him?"

"Come on! You can't be serious!"

"Why not?"

"*Moses?*"

"A man of very strict morals. Strikes me as the Old Testament type. We know by his own admission that he will strike out when provoked . . ."

"Holy cow!"

"*Both* he and Angela were keen, first to tell us nothing, and then to send us off after Akachukwu. Think it through: he's been hiding out, but he misses his woman, so late that night he comes home. But instead of finding her alone, asleep in bed, he finds her up, with two young men, drunk, at three in the morning . . . Is it so unbelievable?"

She was gaping.

I ignored her. "But hang on there, Little Grasshopper, what about Luis? Didn't we wonder right from the start why the killer left him alive?"

Now she looked horrified. "So who shot *him*?"

"You never came across somebody so crazed with passion that they kill the object of their rage, and then shoot themselves?"

She flopped back in her chair. "What are you doing?"

"Just showing you that there is *always* another suspect."

She looked distressed. "Is this what it's like in your head all the time?"

I smiled and reached for my phone, which had started ringing. "Eat your pizza and drink your beer, or you'll never grow up to be strong and smart like me. Stone!"

The last bit I said into the phone.

"Detective Stone, this is Detective Anthony D'Adamo, of the Forty-Fifth Precinct. Do you have two witnesses staying at Prentiss Avenue, in Edgewater Park?"

I frowned at Dehan. "Yes, I do. Why?"

"One Moses Johnson and Angela Rojas?"

"Yes, what's this about, Detective?"

"I think you'd better get over here. They've both been murdered."

————

DETECTIVE D'ADAMO WAS WAITING for us beyond the yellow tape, at the top of the stairs we had so recently climbed to meet Moses Johnson. We moved through a horseshoe of patrol cars and flashing lights and climbed those steps again. He was taller, younger, and thinner than he'd sounded on the phone, and he was smoking a cigarette. He watched us arrive, took a cursory glance at our badges, and said, "So is this your case or mine?"

I sighed. "That's a good question, Detective. Mind if we take a look?"

He shrugged. "Be my guest."

We stayed by the door because the crime scene team were dusting and photographing, and Frank was kneeling beside Angela. She was on her back, at the far end of the room, by the sofa, with her left leg out straight and the right one bent at the knee, flopped over to one side.

Moses was closer. He was lying partially on his left side, with his right arm slightly outstretched, as though he had been reaching for something. I figured he'd been reaching for Angela, trying to get back to her, and I felt momentarily guilty about the way I had teased Dehan earlier. She stood by my side and muttered, "I guess it wasn't him, huh, Stone?"

I nodded. "I guess."

Frank stood and walked over to us. He looked depressed.

I said, "Thirty-eight?"

"Yes, John, a thirty-eight. Seven shots, two in Moses' chest. One in the heart, the other on the right side of his chest. The other five are distributed around Angela's thorax: one in the heart, another narrowly missed the heart, one in her liver, one through the gut, the other in the right lung."

"Cowboy."

"You might say so, John. Please catch this killer."

"Detective D'Adamo wants to know if it's our case or his."

"I need to get this couple back to the lab, but on the face of it, John, these two were killed by the same man who killed Sebastian and shot Luis. I'll ask Joe to do me a favor and put a rush on the ballistics, but you and I both know what we're going to find."

He stared at me a moment, then turned and went back to Angela. Outside, I heard a gurney being rattled up the steps. The door opened, and a young man and a girl with a ponytail maneuvered the trolley through the door and across the floor toward Angela.

Dehan said, "They were sitting on the sofa. Somebody called at the door. They both stood. Angela stayed there, where they'd been sitting. Moses came to see who it was. Whoever it was came in. The lock isn't forced, so maybe Moses let him in? Whatever the case, once in, he shot Moses to get him out of the way, then shot Angela. His rage was against Angela, not Moses. She was the intended victim."

I turned and went out to D'Adamo. I spoke to him while I inspected the door. "Was the lock picked?"

"Uh-uh. Looks like they let the killer in."

"Moses."

"Yup."

Dehan came out. I stood. "Moses opened the door to the killer while Angela stayed inside. But Moses is halfway across the floor. So he went in ahead. The killer followed. At this point, Moses does not feel threatened. But he stops and turns. Now he detects a threat. The killer shoots him twice, almost point-blank,

Moses falls, and his last act before death is to reach for his wife. The killer then closes in and empties the last five rounds into Angela."

D'Adamo nodded. "Sounds about right. I guess it's your case. We're canvassing the neighbors in case anybody saw or heard anything. We'll get statements from anyone who did and send them over to you."

I nodded. "Sure, I appreciate that."

He went down the stairs and talked to the sergeant, then got in his car and left. Behind us the door opened and the girl with the ponytail backed out ass-first. We were in the way, so I touched Dehan's arm and we walked down, back to my car. I sat on the hood, and she stood with her arms crossed, looking at me. Her expression said she didn't think I was very funny.

"Devil's advocate aside, Stone, there is only one person who could have done this—who could have any motive at all to do this."

"I agree." I studied her face a moment. "What motive?"

She spread her hands and shrugged her shoulders like I was being stupid. "He lied, Stone! I'm willing to bet it wasn't the first time in his life that he lied. I knew her, remember? Not intimately, not as well as my mom did, but I knew her. She was a nice, smart woman." She was shaking her head as she spoke. "Frankly, I can't see a woman like that falling in love with a piece of . . . *shit* like him!"

I made a doubtful gesture with my head. "She wouldn't have been the first nice, intelligent woman to fall in love with an odious son of a bitch."

She smiled. "An odious son of a bitch? You have a way with words, Stone."

"I'm serious. Nice men like me are constantly astonished at the way nice women like her fall in love with . . ."

I gestured with my hand and she filled in the blank. "Odious sons of bitches like him. Okay, I grant you it happens. But in this case, it makes a lot more sense that she didn't. He became obsessed with her. I'm willing to bet it all played out pretty much the way he described it, Stone, except that he fantasized her love and her agreement. And when he'd finished his case, he went 'round to her house and she blew him off. He . . ." She shook her head, lost for a moment for words. "He's like a spoiled four-year-old, who flies into a tantrum when he can't have what he wants. She tells him to get lost and he goes crazy. He rapes her. She fights him and he either kills her during the rape, or he kills her afterwards when she tells him she is going to report him to the cops."

I made a face and crossed my own arms. "It's a very credible scenario, Dehan. But it leaves a couple of things unanswered . . ."

"Such as?"

"Well, for one, why did he kill Sebastian and nearly kill his own son?"

She walked away from me and stood staring at a giant pine tree that was casting a dark pool of shade on the blacktop. She repeated my question, as though she knew there was a wise old owl hiding in the tree who was going to give her the answer.

"Because his obsession with Rosario was transferred onto her daughter. He believed that Angela and Sebastian were having an affair and his jealousy . . ."

She trailed off.

I thought about it. "It's not as crazy as it sounds, Dehan, but have you any evidence for it?"

"Not a shred."

"The problem is, Little Grasshopper, that *nobody* has a motive to kill Sebastian. Nobody has a motive to kill either of the boys. Somebody had a motive to kill Angela, and by the looks of it a very strong motive. That motive was rage and hatred . . ."

She was nodding lots before I had finished. "And the one person who is *full* of that kind of rage and hatred is Ed! Okay, not toward Angela maybe, but toward her mother—very possibly! Is it so hard to believe that over the years he has found some crazy-ass reason for transferring that rage onto Angela?"

"No." I had to admit it wasn't.

"Come on, Stone. You have to grant me this one! It's clear. You said from the start there had to be a connection between the Rosario case and Sebastian's case. Here it is: his transferred rage from her mother, for rejecting him, to her daughter. Hell, Stone, if he is crazy enough, and I believe he is, he may even have been raging against the two boys for even being at that house with Angela while she was alone, at that time of the morning. Remember she made them phone? His big beef was that Sebastian was leading his own son astray."

She suddenly pulled her cell from her pocket and dialed a number. After a moment, she snapped, "Yeah, this is Detective Carmen Dehan . . . Yeah, hi, listen, I need you to run a check for me on the handgun owners database . . . Okay, Eduardo Irizarry, of Herring Avenue in Morris Park, the Bronx . . . Sure, I'll hold."

She paced up and down for a minute, watching her feet and kicking tiny stones. After three or four minutes she stopped dead, listening. "He does?" She nodded. "Thank you."

She turned to me. "You *have* to give me this one, Sensei. He is a member of the Pistol Club. He owns a Colt Desert Eagle forty-five, and a Smith and Wesson Bodyguard. That's a thirty-eight. They were *at* the hospital. It's obvious. He followed them home and shot them."

I looked at her for a long while, then spread my hands. "Okay, Dehan, I give you this one. Let's go and pull him in. See if we can make him confess."

"You don't believe it, do you?"

I shook my head. "I didn't say that. I just think the motive is shaky, and there are a couple of minor details that remain unanswered. But you know what? I felt like this was your case from the start. I think it's appropriate that you should close it."

She raised a devastating eyebrow at me and we climbed in the Jag.

# TWENTY-THREE

MARY IRIZARRY OPENED THE DOOR TO US, AND HER mobile, expressive face went through pleasant surprise, confusion, and worry all in a matter of one and a half seconds. Then she said simply, "Detectives . . ." like she'd opened a box and that's what she'd found there. I let Dehan do the talking.

"Good afternoon, Mrs. Irizarry. Is your husband at home?"

"Well, no! He had to go and attend to some things."

"Do you know where he went?"

Unconsciously, her fingers touched her lower lip. "No . . . He doesn't usually . . . Can I give him a message?"

I said, "Mrs. Irizarry, may we come in for a moment? We need to ask you a couple of questions." She hesitated. I smiled and added, "We are very close to catching the person who shot your son, but we need a little help."

"Of course, please come in."

She led us through the ghastly aberration that should have been her home and, once more, into the kitchen. As she walked ahead of us, she spoke. "I hope I *can* help you, I don't really *know* anything. He should be back soon. Can I get you some tea or coffee . . . ?"

It was all delivered as an unthinking stream, like a woman

anxiously seeking the best way to serve. We sat once again around the table where we had so recently delivered to her the news of her son's shooting. I studied Dehan's face and knew that she had had the same thought, because now she hesitated before speaking.

"How long ago did your husband go out, Mrs. Irizarry?"

Mary gave a small laugh. "Oh, he didn't exactly go out. He left while we were at the hospital."

"Perhaps you had better tell us exactly what happened, and what he said."

Mary drew a deep breath and held it a moment while she thought, gazing at the large, silver fridge. "Well, Angela and Sue arrived, with . . . um . . . Angela's friend . . ."

"Moses."

She nodded. "Moses. And you took Ed away to talk about business. And I suppose half an hour later or thereabouts, he came back. He stayed for about ten minutes, then he gave Luis a kiss and said he had to go and attend to some business, and he left."

Dehan thought for a moment. "He didn't say anything about where he was going?"

"No." She smiled. "Ed never really discusses his business with us."

Dehan leaned forward, placing her elbows on the table, and looked hard at Mary. "Please think very carefully before answering this, Mrs. Irizarry. It could be very important. What was being discussed in the room immediately *before* he left?"

Mary's face went completely blank. "Oh, well . . . um . . ."

Dehan sighed. "Did either Angela or Moses mention where they were living?"

She frowned. "Yes! Now that you mention it. Luis was worried about Angela, about her being safe. Well, we *all* were, you can imagine! And Moses said that she was staying with him in his uncle's apartment."

"Did he say where that was exactly?"

She blinked down at the floor for a bit. "Yes . . . um . . . It began with a *P*, in Edgewater Park . . ."

I said, "Prentiss Avenue."

Her face lit up. "There you are! You knew all along!"

I smiled at her. "So we did."

Dehan bit her lip and took another deep breath. "Mrs. . . . Mary, your husband owns a couple of guns."

Mary frowned and nodded. "Yes, he does."

"Does he keep them at the house?"

"In his den, locked in a drawer. He has a license. They are legal, and I *know* he registered them under the SAFE Act!"

"I'm sure he did. Do you mind if we have a look at them? It is very important."

She looked uncertain. "Well, I suppose so. I hope he won't be angry."

Dehan leaned forward. "Mary, it could be a matter of life or death."

She stood, and we followed her down a passage that was carpeted wall to wall in thick, red Wilton, and through a heavy wooden door into a mock Castilian office. There was a hand-carved oak desk in the middle of the floor, and she stopped, staring at it, and then turned to face us. "They're in there, but I haven't got a key. He keeps the key in the safe."

Dehan turned to me. Her face was tight. I pulled out my Swiss Army knife and went around to sit in his big black leather chair. I stopped, looked up at Mary. "Top right?"

"Yes . . ."

I folded the knife and put it away. "The key is in the lock." I slid the drawer open and pulled out a wooden case. I placed it on the desk, and Dehan came and stood by my side as I opened it. There was a silver Desert Eagle and an empty space next to it for the Smith and Wesson .38.

Dehan stared at me. There was no triumph in her expression, only anxiety. "Stone, we should have seen this sooner."

Mary was staring at us, from one to the other. "What is it?"

She came and looked into the box, then at our faces. "What does it mean?"

Dehan stared at her a moment. "Mary, if he was distressed, or in trouble, where would he go? Has he got a friend . . . ?"

Mary had gone gray. "In trouble? What kind of trouble?"

"We are not sure yet. Where would he go?"

"Ed hasn't got any friends . . ." Her lip was trembling, her eyes filling with tears. "Maybe his office?"

"Can you call him on his cell?"

"Yes!" She fumbled in her pocket, pulled out her phone, and dialed his number. She gazed at us in turn. "It's switched off."

"Mary, we are going to look for Ed. If he should come back here, I need you to call us straightaway, you understand?"

She gripped Dehan's hands. "What's going on, Detective Dehan? What has he done?"

Dehan went to speak, then stopped, then shook her head. "We don't know yet, Mary. We just really need to find him. I need a recent photograph, and what car does your husband drive?"

She stared at us, fighting the tears. "A dark blue Audi 8 . . ."

We made our way out into the midday sun again. As Dehan climbed into the Jag, she was calling the precinct. I made a quick call of my own, then got in after her, fired up the big, old engine, and we pulled away. She was saying, "I need an unmarked car on the Irizarry house and an APB on Eduardo Irizarry. I'm sending you a photograph now. He drives a dark blue Audi 8, license plate . . ."

She finished giving the details and hung up. Then she sat staring around her as we moved northwest along the Cross Bronx Expressway.

"Where are we going?"

"I think I know where he is."

She was quiet for a moment. Then, "You going to tell me?"

"I think he's at Rosario's house."

"*Angela's* house?"

I shrugged. "If you like, but to him it's Rosario's house."

"How do you know this? That he's there?"

"You heard him. She is the reason behind all of this."

She raised that devastating eyebrow at me again. "Isn't that a little romantic, Stone?"

I smiled. "Maybe I'm more romantic than you think."

She snorted. "Yeah, right. Whatever. Question is, is he?"

I glanced at her. "The man who fell in love with Rosario because she disagreed with him with that fire and passion that only a Latina can have? I'd say so. Romantics can be arrogant, conceited, and obnoxious, Dehan. I should know."

She shrugged, then after a bit she smiled too. "Okay. It's as good a place as any to start."

"Have I ever led you astray?"

"Only once that I can think of."

I didn't ask.

Twenty minutes later, we pulled up in front of Angela's house. I killed the engine, and we sat for a couple of minutes looking at the green, peeling door with the yellow police tape still hanging forlornly across it. The dark windows looked lifeless. Dehan shook her head. "You sure about this?"

I got out and climbed the nine steps to the porch and examined the lock. It didn't look as though it had been tampered with. I peered in through the window. There was a faint glow from a small backyard, but nothing else. For the second time in a short while I pulled out my Swiss Army knife, selected the screwdriver, fit it into the lock, and gave it a firm thump with my fist. I fiddled a moment and the door opened. I pocketed my knife, lifted the tape, and stepped into the dingy, shabby hall.

The living room was empty and silent. Dehan stared around. I wondered if she was remembering being there with her mother and Rosario. I guessed she was. She looked at me, and her face said she wanted to leave.

"He isn't here, Stone."

"Maybe."

I climbed the stairs. I didn't try to be quiet. The bathroom was empty, and so were the bedrooms. Knowing that Moses and Angela were dead somehow made the rooms feel emptier, more quiet, more still.

I went into the back bedroom and stood at the window, looking out. Dehan was in the doorway behind me, watching me. Her voice sounded odd, disembodied in the gloomy room.

"It's okay to be wrong, Sensei."

"Sure, I know."

"He's not here."

"He is."

"Where, Stone?"

I smiled. "In the backyard. He's sitting there, having a beer."

I could see him from where I stood, sitting in a deck chair on a small patch of lawn. He had a bottle of beer in his hand and the .38 on his lap. He was staring up at the trees and at the sky.

Dehan appeared by my side and stared down at him. "Son of a gun . . ."

"He knows we're here. I made sure he heard us." I turned to face her. "Trust me, Dehan, let me go first, please, and don't pull a gun on him."

She seemed to examine my face, then nodded once. "Okay."

We went down and I stood for a moment in the kitchen door, watching him. Dehan was behind me. I said, "Hello, Ed." He looked at me but didn't say anything. "Is it loaded?"

He took a swig. "There's beer in the fridge. You going to join me?"

"Maybe in a minute. You didn't answer my question."

"Of course it's loaded. What's the use of an unloaded gun?"

"What I'm wondering right now is, what is the use of a loaded gun?"

He shrugged. "I haven't decided yet."

"You planning to shoot me, or my partner?"

He chuckled. "That's all I need, to be convicted as a cop killer. That would be the ultimate triumph of the establishment, wouldn't it? 'We always knew he was a damn criminal! Just goes to show, when the chips are down, you can only trust a white man!'"

"I didn't say that."

"You didn't need to. You set me up, you framed me, you got me."

I stepped down from the door onto the patio flags. Another two steps took me to the edge of the lawn. I could feel Dehan behind me, leaning on the doorjamb.

"The weapon isn't going to help, Ed. It doesn't look good, you sitting there with it in your lap."

He sighed and looked down at the beer bottle in his hand. "I'm sorry, Detective Stone, but that's where it's going to stay. I am licensed to carry it, and frankly, right now I feel threatened."

I looked around for somewhere to sit. There was a low wall that framed the lawn along the patio and the right border, and held assorted flowerpots. I sat there, on the right where I could see Ed's face. I watched him a moment as he watched me back with dark, hating eyes.

"You've won enough trials over the years, Ed, to know that the system is not as corrupt as it used to be. Your big, mock rococo house in Morris Park is evidence of that, your Audi 8 is evidence of that."

He snorted. "Where would I be living, what would I be driving, Detective Stone, if I had been a white Anglo-Saxon protestant?"

"I'm not going to play that game with you, Ed. I am not a threat, neither is my partner. If you are not guilty, you will not go down for this. Just put the gun away, and let's talk."

He puffed out his cheeks and blew. "The gun stays. By all means, let's talk, but your time is limited. I am done. I'm through." He looked at me and I was in no doubt that he was serious. "There is just one way I leave this house, and that's in a body bag."

# TWENTY-FOUR

The ringing of the doorbell made him frown and look toward the kitchen. Dehan raised an eyebrow at me. I said, "It's Susanne Mackenzie. Would you mind showing her through, Dehan?"

She frowned. "You knew she was coming?"

I nodded. She sighed, turned, and disappeared into the house. Ed was scrutinizing me like he'd decided I wasn't human, but he wasn't sure what kind of species I was. Finally, he said, "Susanne?"

I nodded again.

He said, "Why?"

I shrugged with my eyebrows and my shoulders. A moment later, there was a presence at the kitchen door. Sue was there with Dehan behind her. She stared at Ed, who scowled back. Then she turned and stared at me. She looked distressed.

"Detective?"

"Hi, Susanne. Thanks for coming. Eduardo is in a pretty bad way. I was hoping that you could help him."

She looked startled. "Me? How?"

I pointed at the .38 in his lap. "He is planning to shoot himself."

Her face went white. "Ed . . . ?"

He looked angrily at me. "What is this, Stone? What are you playing at?"

I thought for a moment. "Well, it seems to me that that was a pretty important time in all your lives. You all had something really important, something you all lost afterwards."

Sue was watching me fixedly. "What? What thing?"

"Hope. For some of you, it was hope for the community you cared so much about. For others, it was hope for your family, your young children . . . Or hope for that newfound love, a love we so rarely find in life. A love capable of making us dream." I smiled, gave a small laugh, and glanced at Dehan. She was leaning on the doorjamb again, frowning at me like I'd gone crazy. I looked back at Ed. "A love capable of making us believe in magic. Back then, fifteen years ago, just before you moved, Ed, each one of the five of you had some kind of hope in your hearts."

He growled, "What in hell are you talking about, Stone?"

I turned to Sue. "It was hard for you, Susanne, because you had lost your husband recently. I believe you loved him very much, didn't you?"

She nodded. "Yes, I did. He was a wonderful man."

"I've been trying to imagine what that must have been like."

She smiled at me. There was tragedy and gratitude in her face.

"I imagine, to begin with, Rosario must have been a source of support. She was kind, loving, and most important of all, she had been there. She knew how you felt."

She moved to the wall where it bordered the patio, and sat. She gazed for a while at the grass, dappled with the shadows of the leaves in the tall trees. "She was good. She was very kind, very humane."

Ed growled, "She was one in a million. One in seven billion."

She glanced at him. I said, "It's probably the worst thing in the world, to lose somebody you love." The same grateful smile again. "It leaves an emptiness that we think we will never be able to fill again." Ed drew breath, went to say something, but subsided into silence with a small grunt. "But you thought you had found somebody, didn't you, Sue?"

She looked startled for a moment. "I? Well, not really . . . not exactly . . ."

I smiled. "You fell in love. Didn't you?"

Her cheeks colored. "Yes, I did. How did you know?"

"I worked backwards. And when I did that, it made sense. When Matt had gone, the man you were so dependent on emotionally, it made sense somehow that you would turn to his best friend, the man who was so dominant in the group, the man whose personality ruled the roost. You fell in love with a man who wasn't yours. You fell in love with Ed."

Ed was staring at us both like the world had gone mad and it was our fault. "*What? Susanne? Me?* What are you *talking about?*"

I shrugged again. "Little comments here and there, I started piecing it together and it made sense. Without realizing it, just by being that alpha male in your group of friends, he was giving you at least some of the support you needed. And I think, at first, that was enough, wasn't it?"

She nodded. "I loved Mary. She was a good friend, simple, kind, a good mother. Our boys were like brothers."

"You would have been content to love him from afar."

"I would."

I looked at Ed, whose eyes were scandalized. "But then, Ed, you went and fell in love with Rosario. And as if that wasn't enough, you bought a house in Morris Park. In two devastating blows, you destroyed the group, broke Sue's heart, and tore her life apart. First her husband, then you, and then her whole life. You left her with nothing."

He was staring at Sue, aghast. She said nothing, just gazed down at the grass. I went on.

"I'm pretty sure you had picked up the signs. Ed told us he made no secret of his feelings for Rosario. But something tells me the tipping point came when she told you herself. I'm guessing she was pretty excited, and because Marta had backed off a bit, you were probably her closest female friend at the time. His big trial was coming to an end, and he was going to leave Mary and marry her. That must have been a knife in your heart."

She nodded, then raised her eyes to meet mine. "I thought I was going to die. The pain was like nothing I have ever felt, even when Matt died. I left, but then I came back that afternoon, knowing he would be there. I knew it would be hell, but I needed to see it. His car was parked out front. He was there such a long time. I thought I was going crazy, knowing what they were doing in there. I cried and cried, until I felt I had no more tears inside me. Then I saw him come out, looking *happy*, looking so . . ." She shook her head, her face eloquent with bitterness and hatred. She hissed the words like a snake, "*In love!* I watched him drive away. Then I climbed the steps, rang on the bell. She opened the door, like him, so full of happiness and joy, her eyes bright, her hair rumpled from sex. We went into the living room and . . . I don't remember what happened next. The next thing I do remember is being on the floor, sitting on her, with my hands around her neck, and my thumbs pressed deep into her throat. Her face was grotesque, purple, swollen . . ." She looked over at Ed. He had gone a ghastly, deathly gray. She said, "If you had seen her then, you would not have loved her."

He began to sob and tremble. I stood and walked over to him. He stared up at me, with pleading, sobbing eyes, like he was begging me to tell him it wasn't true. I reached down and took the gun from his limp fingers.

As I sat again on the wall, he said, "Why, Susanne? Why? She loved you. She loved us all!"

"But I loved *you*. And all you could see was her. We were happy, the four of us. And then she came along and took over. I hated her for that."

I sighed. "So for the second time in your life, you had this big, empty space. But you were lucky in one thing, weren't you?"

She nodded.

"Your son. Handsome, brilliant. I bet not a day went by that you didn't see Matt looking at you through his eyes."

She was staring down at the grass again, smiling, lost among the reflections of the past.

"But there was one thing, wasn't there? His friendship with Luis you could just about handle, but his friendship with Angela, that must have been tough, especially as they started growing up, moving into puberty, becoming young adults."

She spoke without any real emotion. She said, "She was very like her mother. So pretty, so sweet-natured . . ."

"Did you warn him to stay away?"

She nodded. "He got angry. We started having rows. He told me he couldn't wait till he could afford to move out. That hurt me."

"You know he had a girlfriend, right?"

She gave a small snort and pointed at Ed. It was an oddly humorous gesture. "*He* was married! It doesn't stop them. When they decide to go away, they go away . . ."

"So Friday night he called, in the wee, small hours. He was drunk, he was at Angela's, and he planned to stay there the night. It must have been building up over time, like Rosario's ghost rising up from the dead, to steal yet another one of the men you loved and depended on emotionally. What happened? Where did you get the gun?"

"It was Matt's. He and Ed both felt it was important to be able to protect their families."

"An automatic, right? With seven rounds in the magazine." She nodded, and out of the corner of my eye I saw Dehan put her hand over her eyes, then thump her forehead with the heel of her hand. I went on. "You went up there intending to get Sebastian and bring him home. At least, I'm willing to guess that's what you told yourself. I'm guessing you sat in the car for a bit, looking at the house. There was some light in the window, but you were scared to see what you'd find if you went in. It must have been like a weird reenactment of that time fifteen years earlier, when you'd sat there, outside that same house, waiting for Ed to come out."

She heaved a big, deep, shuddering sigh. "I wasn't sure at times whether it was now or then. It was so dark. It was like the whole world had turned dark. I was dark inside. I wanted to go home!" She stared me in the face. "I really did. I wanted to turn around and go home." She shook her head. "But she had my Sebastian. And if I went home, he wouldn't be there. I'd be on my own."

"Sure. I understand. So when you saw her car pull up, that was the solution. You didn't need to go inside. You could kill her right there and then, and collect Sebastian."

She shook her head. "No. It wasn't her. When I started shooting through the window, I saw that it was a man. Two men. I couldn't see their faces. I knew it wasn't her, but I couldn't stop shooting. It was like my hands were shooting on their own. There was so much noise. My head was just full of horrible noise. And when the gun stopped, I knew I had to leave. I knew Angela was still alive. So I got in the car and went home, to wait for Sebastian . . ."

We were all quiet for a while. Ed was staring down at the grass. His eyes were huge and his jaw was slack. Sue was fiddling with her fingers. She looked as though she might start crying. Somewhere I noticed a bird was singing. I looked up. The dome of the sky was vast and very blue, but also a little cold and uninvolved.

"So, you had been phoning the hospital regularly to check on Luis' condition." She nodded. "And when he came out of the coma, you went there to see him. I guess chances were even that Angela would go too, and one way or another, sooner or later, you would find out where she was."

She nodded again. "I couldn't live. I couldn't live knowing that she was still alive, breathing, loving. That family, those two women, have robbed me of everything I have ever loved. I needed to kill her." She looked me in the eye. "And when I did, when I stood over her, and emptied the gun into her, it felt good."

A little earlier, I had noticed Dehan step into the kitchen with her cell phone in her hand, and now I could hear sirens in the distance, but growing closer. Susanne Mackenzie heard them too. She stared at me for a long moment, then she said, "Will you please kill me? Or let Ed kill me? Please?"

I shook my head. "I'm sorry, Susanne. That is the whole point. It just isn't that easy."

# EPILOGUE

THE REST OF THE DAY WAS A BLUR OF ADMINISTRATIVE grind, statements, and paperwork. At eight o'clock that evening, I leaned back in my chair, making each of my vertebrae crack. I yawned, switched off my laptop, and stared at Dehan across the desk. She nodded, stretched gracefully, and killed her computer too.

She flopped back in her chair and smiled at me. "How did you know? It wasn't something you could have known."

I stood and grabbed my jacket. "Nobody had a motive, Dehan. Therefore, the boys were not the target. If the boys were not the target, but they were in Angela's car, it followed that Angela *was* the target."

She sighed and threw her hands in the air. "Sure! You put it like that and it's obvious! But why Susanne?"

I grabbed her jacket and held it open for her to climb into. She raised an eyebrow but stood and obliged. As she slipped in her arms, I said, "There were a couple of things. For a start, I didn't buy the rape scenario. It seemed out of character to me that a woman like Susanne would not report a rape. It seemed to be contrary in every way to everything she stood for. Then, when Ed was confronted with the allegation, he didn't do his usual bluster and fire and brimstone act. He just dismissed it as absurd. You yourself said that he was surprisingly believable. So then I put two and two together."

We stepped out into the balmy June evening. Above our heads, stars were beginning to glimmer in a turquoise sky. We climbed into the Jag, lowered the windows, and headed toward Morris Park. I was waiting for her to ask me where the hell I thought I was going, but she didn't. Instead, she said, "You put two and two together, and . . ."

I shrugged. "Okay, the assumption was that Rosario was raped and murdered. But then it turned out that Ed *had* had sex with Rosario, but it was consensual. That means that *immediately after* they had sex, somebody murdered her . . . That's pretty odd. And here's Susanne telling us she was raped by Ed. It began to look to me awfully like she was trying to frame him for Rosario's death. Once I saw that, everything else started to fall into place."

She frowned. "Wait a minute . . . She accuses Ed of raping her when he hadn't, so that we would think of him as a rapist in connection with Rosario . . ."

"Correct. But we found out Rosario had not in fact been raped."

"That's deep."

"She is a very deep woman. For her, the murder of Rosario, her own son, and Angela, were all a single act: the destruction of a woman who was trying to steal her loved one." I sighed. "And then there were a few other little things. For example, neither Akachukwu nor Ed could have shot Sebastian. Akachukwu was an experienced, battle-hardened mercenary. His grouping would have been tight and accurate. And as you found out this morning, Ed is a member of the Pistol Club. Frank told us from the start, whoever did the shooting was not accustomed to firing a gun. It was only a thirty-eight, but it was dancing all over the place. There was no grouping at all." I glanced at her. She was nodding. "Same thing with Moses and Angela. At point-blank range, there was a foot between one shot and another."

"Yeah, you're right. I should have thought of that."

"The other thing, which you realized in Angela's garden—I saw you slap your forehead—was that Ed's gun, the Smith and Wesson Bodyguard, is a revolver, and it carries only five rounds. That would have meant that in both shootings, Sebastian and Angela, he would have emptied the cylinder, reloaded, and then fired two more shots. That would have been pretty eccentric, even for Ed. So, when you put that together with the poor aim, Ed just didn't fit the bill, but Sue did."

We were moving along Morris Park Avenue and she still hadn't said anything. She gazed out the window at the deepening dusk and the warm glow from the shop fronts and the windows, with the wind whipping her hair across her face.

"So when I was dragging us off to look for Ed, you called her."

I nodded. "I was pretty sure he was going to go to Rosario's house. Contrary to you, I think he is a very passionate, romantic man, who just happens to be an asshole as well. I had a hunch he was going to want to end it all where she had died. So I asked her to meet us there. It struck me that bringing them together like that might trigger a confession."

I turned into Haight Avenue and after a short drive came to a stop in front of my house. I climbed out and went around to the passenger side, where Dehan had climbed out too. She was giving me an odd look that was masking a smile.

"You're going to force me to eat that damned bison steak whatever happens, aren't you?"

I didn't smile. I was serious.

"Dehan, I owe you an apology."

She frowned. "You do?"

"In Goa, I was an ass, and I am sorry."

She blinked. She was startled.

I went on, "There is something I should have done, and I have a confession to make."

"Stone? Are you okay . . ."

The last word came out muffled because I had taken her in my arms and kissed her. At first it was like kissing a wooden plank. But when I whispered my confession in her ear, she went soft and put her arms around my neck, and we stood there, holding each other, home at last, as the moon rose over the Bronx and smiled.

**Don't miss FIRE FROM HEAVEN. The riveting sequel in the Dead Cold Mystery series.**

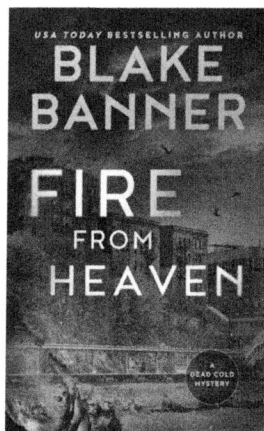

Scan the QR code below to purchase FIRE FROM HEAVEN.

Or go to: righthouse.com/fire-from-heaven

*NOTE: flip to the very end to read an exclusive sneak peak...*

# DON'T MISS ANYTHING!

If you want to stay up to date on all new releases in this series, with this author, or with any of our new deals, you can do so by joining our newsletters below.

In addition, you will immediately gain access to our entire *Right House VIP Library,* which includes many riveting Mystery and Thriller novels for your enjoyment!

righthouse.com/email

*(Easy to unsubscribe. No spam. Ever.)*

# ALSO BY BLAKE BANNER

Up to date books can be found at:
www.righthouse.com/blake-banner

**ROGUE THRILLERS**
Gates of Hell (Book 1)
Hell's Fury (Book 2)

**ALEX MASON THRILLERS**
Odin (Book 1)
Ice Cold Spy (Book 2)
Mason's Law (Book 3)
Assets and Liabilities (Book 4)
Russian Roulette (Book 5)
Executive Order (Book 6)
Dead Man Talking (Book 7)
All The King's Men (Book 8)
Flashpoint (Book 9)
Brotherhood of the Goat (Book 10)
Dead Hot (Book 11)
Blood on Megiddo (Book 12)
Son of Hell (Book 13)

**HARRY BAUER THRILLER SERIES**
Dead of Night (Book 1)
Dying Breath (Book 2)
The Einstaat Brief (Book 3)
Quantum Kill (Book 4)
Immortal Hate (Book 5)
The Silent Blade (Book 6)
LA: Wild Justice (Book 7)

Breath of Hell (Book 8)
Invisible Evil (Book 9)
The Shadow of Ukupacha (Book 10)
Sweet Razor Cut (Book 11)
Blood of the Innocent (Book 12)
Blood on Balthazar (Book 13)
Simple Kill (Book 14)
Riding The Devil (Book 15)
The Unavenged (Book 16)
The Devil's Vengeance (Book 17)
Bloody Retribution (Book 18)
Rogue Kill (Book 19)
Blood for Blood (Book 20)

**DEAD COLD MYSTERY SERIES**
An Ace and a Pair (Book 1)
Two Bare Arms (Book 2)
Garden of the Damned (Book 3)
Let Us Prey (Book 4)
The Sins of the Father (Book 5)
Strange and Sinister Path (Book 6)
The Heart to Kill (Book 7)
Unnatural Murder (Book 8)
Fire from Heaven (Book 9)
To Kill Upon A Kiss (Book 10)
Murder Most Scottish (Book 11)
The Butcher of Whitechapel (Book 12)
Little Dead Riding Hood (Book 13)
Trick or Treat (Book 14)
Blood Into Wine (Book 15)
Jack In The Box (Book 16)
The Fall Moon (Book 17)
Blood In Babylon (Book 18)
Death In Dexter (Book 19)
Mustang Sally (Book 20)

A Christmas Killing (Book 21)
Mommy's Little Killer (Book 22)
Bleed Out (Book 23)
Dead and Buried (Book 24)
In Hot Blood (Book 25)
Fallen Angels (Book 26)
Knife Edge (Book 27)
Along Came A Spider (Book 28)
Cold Blood (Book 29)
Curtain Call (Book 30)

**THE OMEGA SERIES**
Dawn of the Hunter (Book 1)
Double Edged Blade (Book 2)
The Storm (Book 3)
The Hand of War (Book 4)
A Harvest of Blood (Book 5)
To Rule in Hell (Book 6)
Kill: One (Book 7)
Powder Burn (Book 8)
Kill: Two (Book 9)
Unleashed (Book 10)
The Omicron Kill (Book 11)
9mm Justice (Book 12)
Kill: Four (Book 13)
Death In Freedom (Book 14)
Endgame (Book 15)

# ABOUT US

Right House is an independent publisher created by authors for readers. We specialize in Action, Thriller, Mystery, and Crime novels.

If you enjoyed this novel, then there is a good chance you will like what else we have to offer! Please stay up to date by using any of the links below.

Join our mailing lists to stay up to date --> righthouse.com/email
Visit our website --> righthouse.com
Contact us --> contact@righthouse.com

facebook.com/righthousebooks
x.com/righthousebooks
instagram.com/righthousebooks

# EXCLUSIVE SNEAK PEAK OF...

**FIRE FROM HEAVEN**

# CHAPTER 1

IT WAS SUNNY AND WARM, SO WE HAD THE WINDOWS down in the Jag. We were following East Tremont all the way down to the East River. East Tremont is a very long avenue, so we were relaxing and cruising. Occasionally I would glance at Dehan. She was smiling behind her mirrored aviators, with strands of hair whipping across her face.

"Talk me through it," I said.

"Well, as I see it"—she showed me a lot of teeth—"you're Agent Mulder and I am Agent Scully . . ."

"Be serious. We're almost there."

"Be serious?" She raised an eyebrow. "Okay. Danny Brown, aged twenty, found dead at the south end of Soundview Park, near the mouth of the Bronx River, on Monday, the eighth of June, 1998. Cause of death . . ." She fingered some strands of hair from her mouth and tied her hair into a knot at the back of her head. "The ME was unable to establish a cause of death because the body . . ." She raised her shades onto the top of her head like a medieval visor so that she could squint at me. ". . . had been incinerated from his ankles to his neck. I don't get that."

"Just keep going. We'll have a chance to review the details."

She sighed. "Okay. His feet were not burned. They were standing, facing the river, in a pair of flip-flops."

I raised an eyebrow. "Thongs."

She shook her head. "No, Stone. A thong is something else. We have been over this. We are going to call them flip-flops."

I grunted. "There was some burning around the ankles, but the *thongs* were unmelted, despite the heat needed to incinerate the body."

"Who's talking who through this?"

"Whom. You are. Me. You are talking me through it. Continue."

"The ME said that the legs had been severed at the ankle with surgical precision. There was no damage to the cartilage or the joints, other than the singeing. The same was true of the head. This was lying on the grass about eighteen inches from the body, as though it had rolled. There was singeing on the cut, which was also surgical in precision, and there was no damage to the vertebrae—again, other than singeing. Finally, the genitals had also been surgically removed—or at least removed with surgical precision . . ."

"Correct. Good. We do not know that they were surgically removed, only that they were removed, in a way we do not know, with surgical precision."

"That was my point, Stone. That's why I said it."

I grinned at her. "Good."

"They too were singed and placed roughly in the correct position. The rest of his body was ash, with a few pieces of bone."

I nodded. "Those bones corresponded to . . ."

She interrupted. "I was coming to that." She closed her eyes. "Pieces of rib, collarbone, upper arm, thigh, and tibia, suggesting the body had not burned at an even temperature. However, all the bits of bone were found in the correct location on the body. That would be consistent with the body's having burned *in situ*."

I turned right into Schurz Avenue, opposite the Marina Del Rey, and asked, "Problems with that possibility?"

"Well, for a start, the heat needed to incinerate a body to little more than ash, in an open location, like a park, would be insane. Generating that kind of heat in a park would be almost impossible, plus, that kind of heat should have burned his feet, his head, and his balls, and all the grass around him."

"Unless . . . ?"

She sighed. "Unless it was a laser. Which we both know it wasn't."

"I don't know that and neither do you."

She ignored me. "Also, it rained on Sunday night, but there were no footprints approaching or leaving the location where the body was found. Stone, you cannot seriously be considering . . ."

"I am not seriously considering anything at the moment, Little Grasshopper. My mind is open. All I know, like Mr. Socrates, is that I know nothing."

I turned right again into Brinsmade Avenue and pulled up outside Detective Arnaldo Ochoa's house. It was a redbrick box with a front lawn enclosed by a tubular metal fence with chicken wire stretched across it. All in all the effect was ugly, but he obviously took pride in his garden, because that was well tended, with a handsome chestnut on one side and a small vegetable patch on the other.

He came out to greet us before we'd reached the door. He was a friendly, smiling guy who looked unnaturally boyish for his sixty-two years of age. There was a kind of eagerness to his eyes when he smiled, as though he really wanted you to smile back. He held out his hand. "Stone, son of a gun, how're you doing? You still the man at the precinct? I thought you'd be captain by now!"

I shook his hand. "Arn, this is my partner, Carmen Dehan. She's the one who stopped me making captain. Everybody hates her."

He laughed. She didn't. "Come on out back, we'll have more privacy there. What can I get you? Lemonade? Beer?"

He led us out to a backyard that was as well tended as the front. He had a small patio with a garden table and chairs sitting in the dappled shade of a plane tree. On the table there was a glass jug of lemonade. He gestured us to a couple of chairs and poured before he too sat. The sun was turning from warm to hot. Somewhere there was a bee getting busy on some flowers, and there was a powerful smell of freshly cut grass.

He shook his head, still smiling. "So you got cold cases, huh?" He turned to Dehan. "Guy was on fire, you know? Real smart, but a bad attitude. Most people didn't like him. But we were okay, right, Stone? I got you. I knew what you were about. You're a good man." He turned back to Dehan. "He's a good man. Am I wrong?"

She gave a slow shrug. "If you like opinionated dinosaurs, he's okay. He gets the job done. What can I tell you?"

He laughed out loud. "She's got your number, Stone. Opinionated dinosaur. That's good." He laughed again and shook his head. "So you're looking at the Danny Brown case. Man, I don't know what to tell you about that. I lost sleep over that case. I never saw anything like it. I brought it home with me. I still have it, and you know what? Sometimes I pull it out and I sit there in the evening, looking at it, going over it. It defies explanation."

I sipped my lemonade. "Tell me about Danny. What kind of kid was he?"

"He was a good kid. Everybody seemed to like him. He'd taken a year out to think about what he wanted to do, and his parents were cool with that. They were a pretty cool couple, progressive, liberal . . . At the time of his death, he was studying law. His grades were okay, he was happy, his parents were happy. But here's the thing." He looked from me to Dehan and back again, then repeated, "Here's the thing. The kid was obsessed with UFOs and with that TV series *The X-Files*. You know the kind of thing—posters on his walls, all the DVDs, he'd watched every episode God knows how many times. Every book and magazine article ever published on the Roswell incident, Area 51, he'd read them all. What I'm saying, a total nerd. His obsession with the subject was what made him take the year out, and it was bringing his grades down from very good to just okay. That was his parents' opinion."

Dehan asked, "Is that what he was doing out in the park at night?"

He nodded. "I think so, Carmen. Especially in light of what happened later."

"What do you mean?"

"Well, the lights . . ."

Dehan frowned at me. She had only read the case file and the case file made no mention of the lights, and I had not mentioned them to her. I said, "Yeah, tell us about the lights."

"I didn't see them, but there were a hell of a lot of witnesses who did. This was on the Sunday night . . ."

I interrupted, "Before the rain had started, or after?"

He looked surprised. "I'm not sure, John. I'd have to check. If it had started, I don't think it could have been heavy, because a lot of people gathered to watch, along O'Brien Avenue and other places, because you could see them for miles! And I don't think they would have done that if the rain was heavy."

Dehan was frowning. "What kind of lights?"

"Well, from the descriptions I have heard, there were flashing lights, red, yellow, blue, some people say green . . ."

She snapped, "Red, blue, and yellow, that's a chopper! And the green is an illusion where the blue and the yellow mix."

He gave a small, apologetic laugh. "Yeah, maybe, and lasers that were projected down into the park, at approximately the spot where Danny's body was found."

She raised an eyebrow, picked up her glass and sipped, and somehow made it all suggest he was out of his mind. He spread his hands. "You can read the reports in the local papers, Carmen. And when you talk to the witnesses they will all tell you. I don't dispute that there may well be a perfectly reasonable explanation, but I wasn't able to find it. And the lights were there. That is a fact."

I said, "So these lights were above the park."

"At first, yeah. Then, according to the testimony of the witnesses, the lights moved out over the East River, there was a flash of light, and they vanished."

"What color?"

He frowned at me. "You sure ask some funny questions, John. Um, I'm not sure. I'll check, but I think it was just white light."

Dehan looked at me like she wanted to slap some sense into me and said, "So what about the body?"

"So, it's seven thirty on Monday morning when we get the call. This woman is out walking the dog in the morning and she finds the body. Fortunately, she managed to get to the dog before it disturbed anything. This is '98, before everybody had cell phones, so she has to hurry home to call it in. We get there with the crime scene guys and the ME and, believe me, there was not a person there who had ever seen anything like it. It was the craziest fuckin' thing I ever saw in my whole career—in my entire *life*! No exaggeration." He looked at each of us in turn. "For a start." He adjusted his ass in his chair and held out his hands like he was framing a shot in a movie. "There's his feet. They're there, on the grass, about shoulder width apart. Just like he's been standing there looking out at the river. And he's still wearing his fucking thongs."

Dehan smiled. "What are they, like, rubber sandals?"

"Yeah, you know, with the bit that goes between your toes. Like they wear in Florida. His fuckin' head is there, and his fuckin' *balls* are there. Everything, you know, in the right place if you know what I mean. And everything else, his neck, his chest, his arms, his hands, his fuckin' legs—*everything*—has been incinerated. It's just fuckin' ash, you know what I'm saying? Ash! Except there were a few bits of bone, but they were all in the right place where they were supposed to be. It was like, and I don't care if you think I'm crazy because now I'm retired so I can be crazy if I want to, it was exactly like he had been standing there and he had been hit—*zap!*—with a laser."

Dehan sighed and shook her head. I scratched my chin. He

raised both hands and nodded a lot. "I know. I know what you are thinking. It was set up to look that way by some nut. Now, I am going to tell you two things. One . . ." He held up one finger and stared at Dehan. "What possible motive could anybody have to set up such an elaborate, difficult murder? I mean, leave aside for now *how* they did it. We can come back to that in a minute. What possible motive? I mean, that kind of scenario, where the killer sets up an elaborate scene like that after the murder, we only find that with serial killers, right? That is the typical scene where you find that kind of staging of the corpse. But can you think of a single other case where we found a body set up like that?"

Dehan grimaced and I shook my head.

He went on, "Well believe me, I have canvassed every single PD from San Diego to Madawaska, and the only cases like it are unsolved cases of either spontaneous combustion or cattle mutilation." He gave Dehan a challenging smile. "So I ain't the only cop who couldn't solve it. These cases do happen, they are investigated by local PDs, sheriff's departments, *and* the FBI, and they don't get solved."

Dehan looked unhappy. I closed my eyes to think. Ochoa went on. "And two, despite the rain that night, *there were no footprints!* So what are we saying? The body was carefully laid out using a sky crane that nobody noticed?" He leaned forward toward Dehan. "The problem you begin to face, Carmen, is that in order to give this a . . ." He used his fingers to make speech marks. "'Logical' explanation, you have to go to such lengths, to such extremes, that the logical explanation becomes more crazy than the illogical one." He flopped back in his chair, smiling and shaking his head. "His body was surgically incinerated. Get that, *surgically incinerated!* Only a laser can do that, and several hundred people saw a laser at *that* location around the time he must have died."

He spread his hands. Dehan looked at me resentfully. "We have maybe a thousand cold cases, and you have to pick this one."

I gave her my blandest smile. "Just because you are murdered by a bad guy from Betelgeuse doesn't mean you're not entitled to justice, Dehan." I turned to him. "What was your impression of the witnesses . . ."

He snorted. "Such as they were. You say witnesses, but the fact is there weren't any. There were several hundred people who saw the lights that night. But nobody saw the killing. His friends and family, the last people to see him alive. They all liked him, they were all real upset, they all struck me as honest people . . ." He gave a knowing laugh. "In as much as anybody is truly honest, right? But most important of all, there was nobody who had anything you could call a motive." He shook his head. "Nobody had means or motive. It was a locked room mystery, out in the middle of the park."

We were silent for a moment. Finally I asked him, "What is your own feeling? Never mind facts or evidence or lack thereof. What does your gut tell you?"

He smiled at me but pointed at Dehan. "She's going to laugh at me. But Donald Kirkpatrick, who knew Danny really well—he was one of the last people to see him alive—he wrote a book about the case. He called it *Heaven's Fire*. And he says that Danny was shot by a UFO, just like we have assholes who go over to Africa and hunt from helicopters. He figures that's what happened to Danny. He was hunted, for game." He made a face and shrugged. It was an almost apologetic gesture. "I have to say, I agree. After twenty years turning this case over and following every conceivable lead, in my expert opinion, Danny Brown was shot, for sport, by an alien."

# CHAPTER 2

STUART AND MAY BROWN, DANNY'S PARENTS, LIVED across the Westchester Creek in Clason Point. They were both retired—he had been an architect and she a schoolteacher—and, though they sounded surprised on the phone, they were happy for us to drop in. We came off the Bruckner Boulevard onto White Plains Road and then took a right onto Lacombe Avenue. Theirs was a big, yellow detached clapboard affair near the corner with Beach Avenue. We pushed through the wrought iron gate and climbed the five steps to their front door. I pressed the bell and heard it buzz inside. The sun was approaching its zenith and it was getting warm. Dehan stared at me while we waited. I said, "It's almost beer time."

She nodded and the door opened.

Stuart Brown was tall and lean. He had short sandy hair turning to gray and balding on top, like a Franciscan monk. He wore a khaki shirt, with an incongruous Christmas tank top over it, and boot cut jeans. He smiled at us, but it was nothing personal. He looked as though smiling was a habit for him, his go-to response.

"Detectives Stone and Dehan?" We showed him our badges and he gestured us in. "Please, come in, but I am sure I don't know how we can help you. *May!*" This last was hollered up the stairs as we crossed the entrance hall toward his living room. "*May! It's the cops!*" He smiled a smile that would have been cheeky in a child but in him looked like retarded adolescence. "Forgive me," he said. "Go right on in and make yourselves comfortable. May will be down in a moment. Can I offer you anything?"

I took a deep breath, in sympathy with his lungs, and said, "Thank you, no, we really won't keep you long."

We entered an open-plan living room and dining room, with a bow window on the right overlooking the street and a set of French doors at the back, in the dining area, overlooking a back-yard. There was a suite of well-used furniture set around a large coffee table, and against one wall in the dining area there was a huge stripped pine dresser. Stuart directed me to sit in a worn, red calico armchair, and Dehan sat on a sofa that was covered in Mexican rugs and bits of newspaper. Feet hurried noisily down the stairs and May Brown came in on short, plump legs that were accustomed to terrorizing noisy classrooms. The rest of her was as short and formidable as her legs, she too had a habitual smile that meant nothing, and, for a moment, I was transfixed by the bizarre image of these two, retired, in each other's company all day, perpetually grinning at each other without meaning it.

"Detective!" she said, reaching for Dehan with both hands. "Don't get up! I'll sit next to you. What is this about? I am fascinated."

Stuart smiled at me. "Welcome to the Age of Aquarius." He turned to his wife, who had sat beside Dehan, grabbed hold of her hand, and was telling her New York needed more strong women, and said, "Darling, this is Detective Stone, Detective Dehan's partner."

She looked at me like I was the unwanted guest at Thanksgiving. "Of course," she said, with big lips and big eyes. I thought she was going to add, "How nice of you to come," but instead she turned back to Dehan and said, "Stuart and I are intrigued, not to say bemused. It has been twenty years! I believe you run a *cold-case* unit . . . ?"

Stuart sat in the armchair opposite me and crossed one long, thin leg over the other. "That suggests that the case is still open," he said. "But, to be honest, to us it is quite definitely closed."

I frowned. "Closed? How could it be? His murderer was never found."

He shook his head, and May stared at me with eyes the color of over-chlorinated swimming pools. "That is absurd. Forgive me for being blunt, Detective, but only the narrow mind of an officious, white male policeman could possibly fail to see what happened to Danny."

I raised an eyebrow at her. "Are you telling me you know what happened, Mrs. Brown? We will consider any explanation that is properly supported by facts."

She waved a small, plump hand at me. "There you go, you see, 'properly supported by facts.'" She sighed. "As far as we are concerned, Detectives, Danny was shot with some sort of energy beam by trans-dimensional beings, or beings from another planet."

I nodded. "I am aware of that theory, Mrs. Brown, but have you anything concrete in the way of facts that I can take to my inspector, so that we can begin extradition proceedings?"

It went straight over May's head. Dehan clenched her jaw and Stuart cocked an eyebrow at me. "We didn't invite you here to mock us, Detective. We are not alone in believing in the presence of trans-dimensional and extraterrestrial beings among us. There are some very eminent minds who accept the possibility."

I nodded. "I'm not mocking you, Mr. Brown, far from it. But I would like you to understand that the NYPD can't just walk away from a homicide investigation because the murder may have been committed by an extraterrestrial."

"Have you read Donald Kirkpatrick's book on the case?"

"No."

"I suggest you do. His investigation is somewhat more thorough than the NYPD's, I am bound to say. His analysis of the situation is profound and comprehensive, and he shows, quite conclusively, Detective Stone, that our son's murder could not have been carried out—mark my words here—*could not have been carried out* by a human being. Once you establish that point, where do you go from there . . . ?"

Dehan scratched her head and spoke. "That's the second time Donald Kirkpatrick's name has come up. What exactly was his relationship to Danny?"

He sank back in his deep chair and brushed some imaginary dust from his blue jeans. "'Relationship' is an unnecessarily strong word, Detective Dehan. They had no *relationship* other than that Donald ran the investigation group in which Danny was involved, along with at least a dozen other people."

I said, "UFOs were a consuming interest for him . . ."

"It was a passion. For May and myself it had been a lifelong interest, but for Danny it was a true passion. We encouraged him but always urged him to approach the subject empirically. Sadly, for the vast majority of ufologists these days, the subject has become religion by another name. And John Mack, for all his good intentions, was, I am afraid, largely to blame."

He said this apologetically, as though I might be scandalized by the suggestion. I shook my head. "John Mack?"

"Professor of psychology at Harvard University, wrote several books on abduction syndrome, concluded that . . ."

"Forgive me, Mr. Brown, we are on the clock and I am sure you have lots to do yourself. What about the other members of the UFO group? How did Danny get on with them? Do any relationships stand out as either particularly good or particularly bad?"

May sighed and shook her head. "Truly, Detective Stone, it is a shame you can't understand you are barking up the wrong tree . . ."

"Help me to understand."

"Danny was gregarious, outgoing, emotionally *very* healthy.

He had all the self-assurance of the only child, which was a deliberate decision on . . ." She nodded graciously at her husband. ". . . our part. The result was that everybody loved him. He was popular, fun, charismatic. He had a *great* sense of humor, didn't he, Stuart?"

Before Stuart could answer, I cut in. "I am sure he was a charming person, Ms. Brown. But, as I am sure you know, the motive for murder lies always in a relationship—whatever the basis of that relationship may be—so at the moment we are keen to understanding all of Danny's relationships. Did he, for example, have a girlfriend?"

She placed both her hands on her lap and affected a loud, parrotlike laugh. "Just one?" She hooted again. "You have photographs of him? He was *gorgeous!* And that happy-go-lucky personality! The girls were crazy about him!" She shook her head. "But he was not ready to settle . . . Hold on."

She rose and strutted on those powerful legs to the dresser in the dining room. There she squatted down with startling flexibility and opened one of the cupboards in the base. She extracted a couple of photo albums and brought them back with her, leafing through the top one as she walked.

She sat next to Dehan and handed her the album. "There, that's him. Was he hot or what?" She wheezed. Dehan studied the photos without expression. May went on, nudging Dehan with her elbow. "'Course, he'd be forty now, a bit too old for you, hey?"

Dehan handed me the album and I looked at a large photograph of about fifteen people against a backdrop of pine trees in what appeared to be a mountainous area. Most of the people there were young men and women, probably in their early to midtwenties, though behind them there was an older man, perhaps in his late thirties. He was the only one who was not smiling. His gaze was more what you might describe as keen. Next to him was a woman, maybe ten years younger than him. She looked Asian, perhaps Filipina. May was saying, "Danny is the one in the middle, sitting at the front, with the open denim shirt."

I found him. He was a handsome young man with a mischievous grin and floppy brown hair. Hunkered down on his left was a powerfully built, dark-haired guy with his arm around Danny's shoulders, and on his right was a pretty girl, laughing, with her head on his shoulder. Danny's arms were both on his knees. I looked up at Stuart, who was watching me carefully.

"May I take a copy of this?"

He gestured at me with an open hand. "Be our guest."

I took a picture on my cell, then showed Stuart the album. "Who are the two either side of him?"

He took it and set it on his lap, gazed at it for a while with sad eyes. "This was their first field trip after he'd joined them. The man standing at the back is Donald Kirkpatrick, a highly intelligent man. Some kind of scientist by training. He founded the group. The two at the front . . ." He took a deep breath, which turned into a sigh. "I remember them, I don't recall their names. May?"

He handed it to her. She glanced but didn't take it. "Paul Estevez and Jane Harrison."

"They look pretty close."

"I told you, everybody loved him, but he was a free spirit. For them it was probably nothing more than a social activity. For him it was a search for the truth. And, as Donald points out, it was a search that cost him his life." She regarded me with an expression that was close to pity. It was only the hint of contempt that stopped it getting there. "Really, Detective, you are asking the wrong questions. What you need to be asking is, what did he discover? What did he unearth that made him a target?"

I spread my hands. "Okay. Tell me. What *did* he discover that made him a target?"

Dehan was watching May with the kind of expressionless face she normally reserved for people she wanted to slap. Before May could answer me, Dehan asked, "A target for whom, Mrs. Brown?

And also, what evidence have you got that he *was* a target for somebody? If you have that evidence, why have you not shared it with the police?"

Stuart had raised his hands in a "slow down" gesture and was smiling at the coffee table. "Hang on, hang on, let's take these questions one at a time. First: we are not withholding any information. Second: we do not have any proof, as you would understand it, that Danny was anybody's target." He spread his hands and nodded. "Beyond the obvious fact that he *was* murdered. Third: we don't know who he was a target for, any more than a herd of gazelles in Africa knows who is shooting at them from the helicopter. However, we are satisfied, based on the evidence we have, which is the same evidence that you have, that Danny was not killed by a human being." He shrugged his shoulders and shook his head in an oddly helpless gesture. "It simply isn't possible." He gazed at me a moment. "And to answer your question, Detective Stone, we don't know what he had unearthed."

"But you think he had unearthed something."

It was May who answered. "Stuart is not convinced, but I am. He would often go off for several days at a time. Sometimes alone, sometimes with members of the group; sometimes it was for a night, sometimes several days at a time. He never told us what he was doing or where he was going. That's why we didn't raise the alarm that weekend. *I* think he discovered something . . ."

Stuart sighed and attempted a smile. "It will sound absurd to you, Detectives. It seems absurd to anyone who has not done the research. But there are very eminent people, in the White House, in the Pentagon, in academia, all of whom are agreed that there *is* a conspiracy to conceal the truth about UFOs. And we think it is possible, May is convinced, that Danny had found something. And whatever it was he found got him killed." Again he shrugged, again he spread his hands in that helpless gesture. "Nobody else had a motive. Nobody else had the *means!*"

I thought about it for a long moment. I was aware of Dehan watching me. Maybe she wanted to slap me too. I pointed at the album, which lay open on the coffee table. "Have you got contact details for Paul and Jane?"

May shook her head. "No, but Donald will have." She reached down by the side of the sofa and picked up a brown leather handbag. From it she extracted a small notepad and a pen. She scrawled an address and a phone number and handed it to Dehan. "He'll be happy to see you."

Dehan took it and thanked her. "One last question before we go. Can you tell us about his movements that night?"

May shook her head. "No. We last saw him on the Friday. They were all going on some kind of field trip, after which they were going to have a party or something at Donald's place. We never saw him again."

We thanked them and stood. They followed us to the door. As Stuart opened it, he held my eye a moment. "The FBI tried to silence us, you know."

I frowned.

Dehan snapped, "The FBI tried to silence you? How?"

He nodded. "They called on the telephone and they came to see us: two men. They'll deny it, of course. But they came and advised us, for our own good, to keep quiet. Don't be surprised if you hear from them. They'll tell you to drop the investigation and close the case."

We thanked them again and stepped out into the midday glare.

# CHAPTER 3

WE DIDN'T GET INTO THE CAR; INSTEAD I WALKED TO the top of Beach Avenue and looked down. Dehan was sitting on the hood of my old, burgundy Jag, watching me. I pointed. "Soundview Park is four or five hundred yards down there. That's where they found him. What do you say we go and have a look?"

She nodded, stood, and followed me. We walked in silence for a while, enjoying the sunshine and the warmth. After a moment, she slipped her arm through mine and leaned against me as she walked.

"Are you buying this alien . . ."

"Don't say BS."

She glanced at me. "So you are buying it?"

"That is a very open question, Dehan."

"What do you mean? It's a yes or no question. Are you buying it? Yes, I am; no, I'm not."

I raised an eyebrow at her, but she looked away, as though she was checking for traffic on an empty road. We crossed Patterson Avenue and continued down Beach toward the park, which was now clearly visible at the end of the road, about a hundred yards away.

"Okay," I said, "what is 'it' exactly? What is it, precisely, you are asking me if I am buying? Are you asking me if I believe that alien life exists on other planets, or moons? If so, I don't believe it, I think it is impossible that it does *not* exist. Are you asking me if I believe alien life forms are visiting Earth? I just don't know, but I know there are some very smart people who do. Or are you asking me whether I believe that Danny was murdered by an extraterrestrial?"

"That one."

"Then the answer is, I don't know who killed him, yet. Statistically he is more likely to have been killed by a human being, over sex or money. But I am not going to make the evidence fit my theory, I am going to develop my theory . . ."

"Based on the evidence, yadda yadda. I know. But come on, Stone! He was shot by an alien with a ray gun? Seriously? And while we chase little green men, the killer pisses his pants laughing and gets away with murder."

We had reached the bend in the road where it becomes O'Brien Avenue. To our right there was an untended wilderness of knee-high grass and flowers interspersed with oak and linden trees. I stopped and she stopped with me. I gazed at it a moment and said absently, "This is what the world *should* look like, Dehan."

She looked at me in surprise and smiled. "Why, John, you're a romantic after all!"

I smiled back and pointed in among the undergrowth. "He was found in there."

We picked our way through a broad border of grasses, wildflowers, and bindweed until we came to a broad expanse of coarse scrub and gray clay, bounded by a path that entered the park from the west, ran along the riverbank for two hundred yards, and then turned north, skirting the amphitheater. I stopped and looked around for a moment, remembering the photos I'd studied. Then I pointed south, to a slight rise where I could see a small tree. "Over there, by that oak tree."

We trudged across the dense, cloying soil for maybe a hundred yards, until we came to a tall, spindly pin oak which twenty years earlier would have been little more than the sapling I had seen in the picture. I stood by the tree and took ten paces to the west, turned, and looked at Dehan, who was watching me with her hands in her back pockets. "This is the spot," I said. "Try to visualize it. Sometime on Sunday night. It's been raining on and off since late afternoon. It's dark. His feet, in his thongs, are here." I found two large clumps of clay and positioned them where his feet had been. "Facing out toward the water. His body, or what is left of it, is lying back from his feet. Imagine," I said, "that a guy with a samurai sword, as sharp as a scalpel, had cut through his ankles, and he had fallen straight back."

"Wait."

She picked up a stick and came over, scratched out the shape of his body, with no head, lying on the ground, with his arms at forty-five-degree angles from his body. Then she went and found a large clump of clay, the size of a melon. "His head is . . ." She gauged the distance with her eye and placed the lump where his head had been found. ". . . about here. And . . ." She grinned, found a twig and two acorns, and placed them where his genitals would have been. ". . . the pièce de résistance!"

I pointed at the ground. "This is clay. It sucks up water, holds it a long time, and keeps its shape."

She nodded. "I hear you. There should have been footprints." She screwed up her face like an angry fist. "But wait, please, let's not get ahead of ourselves, Sensei. Let's look at each step separately and then see if we can fit them together at the end. First, of the people we know of, who had anything like a possible motive?"

I scratched my head. "Anything *like* a possible motive? Any one of them, Dehan. We just don't know anything about his relationships yet. He was attractive, single, wanting to stay unattached. Right there you have a breeding ground for motives: jealousy, rejection, envy . . ."

"Okay, so opportunity." She sighed and corrected herself. "Okay, not opportunity, because we know nothing of his movements, so any one of them might have had opportunity, including his parents."

I nodded. "Which brings us to means."

We stared at each other for a long time. Then she threw her hands in the air and expostulated, "Son of a gun! Means! Sure, anyone with a laser scalpel in 1998! But not just a laser scalpel—a laser scalpel capable of incinerating an entire body at the same time as surgically removing the head, the feet, and the . . ." She sighed. "This is bullshit, Stone." She turned to me. "He was not killed by aliens!"

I chuckled in a way I knew was annoying. "It's not just the scalpel and the incineration, there is also the question of how the killer got here across the wet clay and then left, without leaving any tracks. Even if we argue that Danny might have been killed somewhere else and deposited here, the killer still has to cross the wet clay and lay out the feet, the head . . ." I shook my head. "And then go back. It's a hell of an undertaking."

She made a three-hundred-and-sixty-degree turn, scanning the entire visible park and the river. Then shook her head. I pointed up at the sky. "The lights were seen up there." She stared at me like she was about to smack me. "Don't look at me in that tone of voice, Dehan. The lights were seen by several hundred witnesses, they are a part of the evidence we have to sift through. Suck it up, baby. They were seen directly above the scene, firing lasers down toward the ground. They then moved south for a way and suddenly vanished in a flash of white light."

She turned and pointed at me. "Okay, Stone, I'm going to come at this from a different angle."

"Good."

"Forget the whole UFO thing, right?"

"This is different?"

"Let's face it, if he was killed by an alien, we will never prove it and, as you pointed out to May Brown, we have no extradition treaty with Betelgeuse, so we will never catch him. Therefore the only line of inquiry worth pursuing is, the killer was human."

I shrugged. "The statistics are on your side, at least."

"Shut up and tell me what you think: our killer is smart, he thinks out of the box. He would have to, to come up with a plan like this *and* get away with it. I mean . . ." She gave a small laugh. "If you hadn't pissed off Captain Jennifer Cuevas back in the day, we would never have been assigned to cold cases, and he would have got away with this. And he still might! So he is smart, and an original thinker."

"Can't argue with that."

"And . . ." She raised a finger. "He is daring. He is not afraid to go extreme and take risks."

I raised an eyebrow at her. "Hmmm . . ."

"So, he puts together a drone, or whatever equivalent they had back in the '90s, with all the flashing lights and lasers. He hovers it over the park. It's daring because it is drawing everybody's attention, but it is clever because it also pretty much guarantees that nobody is going to come into the park. Remember, in 1998 *The X-Files* is at the peak of its popularity, as is abduction syndrome. So people are *scared!*"

I made a "you have a point" face and nodded.

She went on, "So then, and this is the really daring bit, he comes in off the river on a hovercraft."

I smiled. "A what?"

"Like the ones they use in the swamps in Florida. If anybody hears the noise they'll think it's the UFO. He positions the body, takes off back into the sound, brings the drone in to land on the craft, and makes off across the river to . . . what? Powell Cove? Little Neck, Kings Point, wherever!"

"It's certainly daring."

"Is it less likely than aliens? Have you got a better theory that doesn't involve *Predator*?"

I shook my head. "I have no theories at all at the moment." I pointed down toward the water. "You have a line of trees between the park and the river. Your hovercraft would have to break through them."

She nodded. "Yes, but over there, down by Harding Park, you have a little harbor with no trees, and he would have access through there."

"That's true." I thought a little more. She danced around with her fists up, like Cassius Clay or Bruce Lee. "C'mon, Stone. Hit me. Show me whatcha got."

"How did he lay out the body without leaving any prints in the mud?"

She thought for a moment. "He settled the hovercraft on the mud, and placed his victim without getting down, lying on his belly on the craft, and then left."

I nodded for a while, visualizing it, then said, "You about ready for lunch?" She nodded vigorously and we turned and started walking back toward Beach Avenue. I said, "It's very good. In fact, I only see two problems with your ingenious scenario, Dehan."

"What?"

"The first is, you are assuming he was killed elsewhere, but you still leave unanswered the question, how did he kill him? The second, and more difficult, is, having laid the corpse out and sprinkled the ash in the form of the body, on leaving, the very powerful fan that the hovercraft uses to move about would have blown that ash all over the park, even wet."

She stopped dead in her tracks and sighed. "Damn it! I should have seen that." She started to walk again. "It does tell us one thing, though. Danny was killed—or the body was placed—after the worst of the rain, because heavy rain would have washed the ash away."

"Yup. That's true. Now we just need a hovercraft that doesn't use a powerful fan."

She shoved her hands in her pockets and eyed me. "You mean like a flying saucer with a dilithium crystal warp drive."

"Don't be downhearted, Dehan. Top of our to-do list, after we've talked to everyone: make a list of vehicles that could have covered that distance, discreetly, and deposited the body without leaving tracks."

"Yeah, makes sense. Also, a list of tools or instruments that could have generated that kind of intense, focused heat over an area of, what, five and a half feet? To cut off his ankles and his head."

I looked at her, chewing my lip as we walked, turning over what she'd said in my head. I knew for a fact that there was no such instrument or weapon. It just didn't exist in terrestrial technology. But I didn't say so.

We came out of the park and made our way up toward my ancient, uncomputerized, primitive brute of a car. There was not a shred of software in it. Even the lock was mechanical. As I slipped the key in the door and opened it, I found that oddly comforting.

Before getting in, I leaned on the roof to look at Dehan, and felt the heat through my sleeve. She leaned on the other side and lifted her sunglasses to squint at me. I said, "Hamburger, beer, Donald Kirkpatrick."

She blinked. "The elegance of your syntax is matched only by the beauty of your words, Sensei."

"I thought so," I said, and climbed in behind the old walnut steering wheel.

Scan the QR code below to purchase FIRE FROM HEAVEN.
Or go to: righthouse.com/fire-from-heaven

Printed in Great Britain
by Amazon